The FINAL REVENGE

An Adventure of Detective Surya

The FINAL REVENGE

An Adventure of Detective Surya

Dr. Prabhat Bhattacharyya

Translated by
Partha Mukhopadhyay

EXCELLER BOOKS®
A GLOBAL PRESS

The Final Revenge
An Adventure of Detective Surya

Cover by Exceller Books using resources from Pixabay.com

ISBN: 978-93-48892-48-5
Published in India in 2025 by Exceller Books,
An imprint of GE Group

Address: G1, Dream Apartment, Degree College Road, Belgharia,
Kolkata, 700056, India
www.excellerbooks.com

EXCELLER BOOKS®
A GLOBAL PRESS

Dedicated to my family members, teachers and patients

Author's Note

The Final Revenge is the second book of the *Detective Surya* series in English. My heartfelt thanks to Team Exceller Books for their dedicated efforts in bringing this book to life in such a fine form. My special thanks to Mr. Partha Mukhopadhyay for undertaking the arduous task of translating the book. His effort in capturing the essence, tone, and nuances of the original work has added immense value to this edition.

I am truly overwhelmed by the response from readers to the first book in the series, *Mysteries of the Green Planet*. **The Final Revenge** is a thriller inspired by the great Indian epic, the *Mahabharata*. Just as in the epic, the cycle of revenge finds its resolution, and at the heart of it all is Detective Surya, with his sharp mind and unwavering presence.

Dhananjaya and Vasudeva were travelling by car, with Vasudeva behind the wheel.

"What's on your mind? You've been sitting there with your hand on your cheek," Vasudeva asked, glancing at him.

"I'm really troubled. Nothing feels right," Dhananjaya replied, his voice heavy.

"What is it? Tell me," Vasudeva urged gently.

Dhananjaya sighed. "What we're about to do... it will cost many lives—some of them our own kin."

Vasudeva's tone sharpened. "After everything they've done, this is what you're worried about? They're the reason we're in this situation. They killed your father, Dhananjaya. And still, you hesitate to take revenge? Then I have nothing more to say."

"No, no—I will take revenge. There's no doubt in my mind," Dhananjaya said firmly. "Now, the game begins."

"Swear it," Vasudeva demanded.

***

Grandfather Bhishma, the commander of the Kaurava army, blew his conch, producing a roar like that of a lion. The war drums resounded loudly. Krishna blew his conch, *Panchajanya*. Arjuna blew his conch, *Devadatta*. Yudhishthira and the others blew their own conchs accordingly.

At Arjuna's request, Krishna drove the chariot between the Kaurava and Pandava armies. Seeing many relatives, teachers, and friends on both sides, Arjuna became distressed. He said to Krishna, "Seeing all these relatives on the battlefield, my body feels weak, and *Gandiva* is slipping from my hands. I have lost all desire for war. I no longer seek victory—how can we enjoy happiness by killing our own kin? Out of greed for the kingdom, we are about to commit a terrible sin. It would be better to die unarmed than to engage in this."

Saying this, Arjuna cast aside his weapons and sat down in the chariot.

Krishna then said to the troubled Arjuna, "In this moment of crisis, stand firm—do not yield to weakness."

"How can I harm the venerable Bhishma and Drona? How can I slay such great sages? A shadow of doubt clouds my mind—I do not know what is right. Please guide me."

Krishna replied, "The wise do not grieve for the living or the dead. Just as a man discards worn-out clothes and puts on new ones, the soul discards a worn-out body and takes on a new one. A steady person is not disturbed by this.

"One who is born must die—there is no reason to grieve over this inevitability. And for a Kshatriya, nothing is more honourable than righteous warfare. If you do not fight, you will abandon your duty and lose your honour. Therefore, cast aside all doubt and engage in the battle—you will not incur sin by doing so.

"Your right is in action, not in the fruits of action. Do not seek the results. Renounce attachment and perform your duty."

Krishna gave Arjuna many more advice and, at Arjuna's request, revealed his *Vishwarupa*, the universal form. Arjuna, overwhelmed with wonder and excitement, folded his hands and said, "O God, I see all the gods, various animals, and all the sages within your body. I cannot see your beginning or end. O God, be pleased! The sons of Dhritarashtra, the kings, Bhishma, Drona, the son of Suta, and our chief warriors are all rushing towards you and entering your terrible mouths. Just as moths rush into a flame for their destruction, similarly, all the worlds are entering your mouths with great speed to meet their end. You are devouring all beings from every side with your blazing form. Tell me, who are you, O fierce one, O Rudra-rupa? Salutations to you! O God of all gods, be pleased. I wish to know you as the original, eternal being."

Then Krishna said, "I am *Kala*, the destroyer of worlds. The warriors who are present here will die even if you do not slay them. I have already killed them—you are merely an instrument. Arise, conquer the enemy, and enjoy a prosperous kingdom."

Arjuna said, "O God, I bow to you a thousand times from all directions. How many times I have addressed you as Krishna, Yadava, and friend—without knowing your greatness—and have mocked you! Please forgive me for all that. Be pleased and assume your earlier form."

Then Krishna returned to his normal form and gave further instructions. He said, "Arjuna, if you think, out of arrogance, that you will not fight, that resolve will be in vain—your nature will compel you to fight. I have already done what must be done. He who does not recognize this, whose intellect is not fixed in action, achieves nothing—even if he kills all. Surrender your heart to Me. Become My devotee and worshipper. Bow down to Me. You are dear to Me, and you will attain Me. Abandon all other duties and take refuge in Me alone—I will free you from all sins."

Arjuna said, "My delusion has been destroyed. Because of you, I have attained true knowledge; my doubts have been dispelled. I will obey your command."

Freed from all doubts, Arjuna prepared for battle. The stage was set for a terrible war.

***

Dhananjaya began gathering weapons. He sought the most powerful ones. Then...

A smile appeared on Vasudeva's face.

***

Ranajoy Sarkar was sitting in his jewellery shop in Boubazar, settling the accounts. He was a renowned jeweller. Suddenly, he was startled by a loud clanging sound—someone had broken the glass behind him. Along with it came a hoarse voice that said, "You will be punished for your sins in two days."

He rushed outside but saw no one. Fear gripped him. Someone had thrown something from outside and shattered the glass. But who? And who had said those ominous words? What sin, and what punishment? His hands and feet began to tremble.

The security guard, Sunil, was talking to someone a little distance away. Ranajoy called out to him.

"What happened, sir?" Sunil asked.

"Come inside and see! You're busy chatting while this happened."

Sunil quickly entered the shop and gasped. "What a disaster! Who could have done this?" He picked up a piece of stone from the floor and added, "Someone threw this and broke the glass. Should I report it to the police, sir?"

"No need. Just clean up the broken glass and speak to Subhankar about installing a new pane."

"Okay, sir."

Ranajoy then closed the shop and headed home to Maniktala.

"Feeling unwell, sir?" the driver asked.

"No, no, it's nothing. Just drive."

He felt a bit better after reaching home.

A widower, Ranajoy lived alone; his son worked in Delhi. The maid and cook came every day.

It could have just been someone throwing a stone—but that voice… whose voice was it? Was his mind playing tricks on him? Possibly.

He forced himself to eat and switched on the TV. He enjoyed watching old Bengali films. A movie titled *Pratishodh* was playing on a channel, but he didn't like it. He turned off the TV and went to bed. That night, he had to take a sleeping pill.

The next morning, he woke up late and made himself a cup of tea. As he sipped it, the doorbell rang. When he opened the door, he found his manager, Subhankar, standing there. Subhankar was honest and efficient.

"Sir, I heard everything from Sunil. Strange incident! Anyway, I've arranged for new glass to be installed," said Subhankar, studying Ranajoy's face. "You look pale."

"It's nothing," Ranajoy replied quietly.

"If you're not feeling well, there's no need to go to the store today. I'll take care of everything," Subhankar offered with concern.

"Alright," Ranajoy nodded.

That day, he stayed home and didn't go to the store.

***

The Kauravas formed a *Chakravyuha* as planned by Dronacharya and began fighting. Then Yudhishthira said to Arjuna's son, Abhimanyu, "We do not know how to break the *Chakravyuha*. Only Arjuna, Krishna, Pradyumna, and you know the technique. I request you to break through this formation."

Abhimanyu replied, "I must enter the *Chakravyuha* immediately. I know how to enter it, but I do not know the method of coming out."

Then Yudhishthira said, "My son, you break through the *vyuha* and create a path for us. We will follow that path and protect you."

Bhima added, "My son, Dhrishtadyumna, Satyaki, and I will follow you, along with many other warriors. Once you breach the formation, we will enter and destroy the enemy army."

With Yudhishthira's blessings, Abhimanyu entered the *Chakravyuha* and began to devastate the Kuru army. Duryodhana, enraged, rushed to stop him. Drona, Ashwatthama, Kripa, Shalya, and others showered arrows on Abhimanyu, but he continued to fight with unmatched valour. Drona was pleased to witness the bravery of his disciple's son.

At Duryodhana's request, the Kauravas attacked Abhimanyu. Duhshasana fell unconscious after being struck by Abhimanyu's arrow. Abhimanyu then engaged in combat with Karna, killing one of Karna's brothers and injuring Karna with his arrows. His attack shattered the massive Kaurava army, causing the warriors to flee.

Abhimanyu created a path into the *Chakravyuha* and entered it. However, Jayadratha, the Sindhu king and Dhritarashtra's son-in-law, blocked the entrance, and Abhimanyu was left alone.

Surrounded by the Kuru army, Abhimanyu continued to fight bravely. He killed Rukmarath, the son of Shalya, and Lakshman, the son of Duryodhana. Furious at the death of his beloved son, Duryodhana ordered that Abhimanyu be killed. The Kaurava charioteers surrounded and attacked him. Following Drona's advice, Karna cut off Abhimanyu's bow from behind and killed his horses and charioteer. The warriors then launched a joint assault. All of Abhimanyu's weapons were destroyed, and he began fighting with a club. At that moment, Duhshasana's son struck Abhimanyu on the head with a mace, and his lifeless body fell to the ground.

Yudhishthira was heartbroken and began to lament Abhimanyu's death. Meanwhile, Arjuna was engaged in battle with the Samsaptakas. After defeating them, he returned to the Pandava camp. Not seeing Abhimanyu, he became anxious and inquired about him. Upon learning of his son's death, Dhanajay was overwhelmed with grief. Krishna consoled him. When Dhanajay heard that no one could help Abhimanyu because Jayadratha had blocked the entrance to the formation, he was filled with rage. He vowed, "I will kill the sinful Jayadratha before sunset tomorrow, or I will enter the blazing fire. No one will be able to save him. Wherever he hides, I will cut off his head."

Arjuna pulled the string of *Gandiva*. Krishna and Arjuna blew their conches, *Panchajanya* and *Devadatta*. The sky, the underworld, and the earth trembled. The Pandavas roared.

Seeing this, Jayadratha was terrified. Duryodhana reassured him, saying, "Don't worry. We will all protect you." Drona also offered him reassurance.

That night, no one in the Pandava camp slept. Everyone was anxious about Arjuna's difficult vow. In the morning, Yudhishthira met with all the warriors. Krishna said to him, "Even if all the gods come to protect Jayadratha, Arjuna will kill him today."

***

Ranajoy finished his lunch and turned on the TV. For the last two days, he had been thinking too much. Maybe it was a minor matter—there was no need to dwell on it so much. So, he decided to feel light-hearted and at one point, fell asleep on the sofa without turning off the TV.

When he woke up, it was evening. He needed some tea. Just then, the bell rang. The cook, Ratna, had arrived. Ranajoy asked her to make some tea.

"Someone came and asked me to give this to you," Ratna said, handing an envelope to him.

"Who gave it to you?" Ranajoy asked.

"I didn't pay much attention," Ratna said.

When Ranajoy opened the envelope, he saw a piece of paper with the words: *Prepare to be punished for your sins*, and he grew worried again.

"Here, take your tea. Today, I'm making *paratha* and *aloor dom*. Okay?"

Ratna finished cooking and left for the day. Ranajoy began pacing around the floor. He could not sit still.

The doorbell rang again. As soon as he opened the door, two people rushed inside and shut the door behind them.

"Who are you?" asked Ranajoy.

"Can you recognize us?" one of them replied.

Ranajoy looked at them carefully.

"You!" he exclaimed, a look of surprise and fear in his eyes.

"Well, you've recognized us then. You must be wondering why we've come to you," one of them asked.

Ranajoy was speechless. He saw one of them loading a bow with arrows.

In a sudden panic, he turned and rushed up the stairs, desperate to lock himself in. But he could not make it far.

An arrow struck him in the back.

As he collapsed face down, he heard, "This is the punishment for your sins."

A sharp cry—and then, it was all over.

***

Drona told Jayadratha, "You will remain behind me with your army, and the other heroes will protect you." Drona then constructed the *Chakrashakata Vyuha*. Behind this formation, a *Garbhavyuha* called *Padma* was built, and between them, a *Suchivyuha* was positioned. Drona stood in front of the *Chakrashakata Vyuha*.

Arjuna initiated the battle. After defeating Duryodhana's brothers, Durmarshana and Duhshasana, he confronted Drona. A fierce battle followed between the two. Then, on Krishna's advice, Arjuna left Drona and proceeded towards Jayadratha. He killed many warriors along the way, and many others fled in fear. Seeing Dhanajay advancing through Drona's formation, Duryodhana came to stop him. A fierce duel broke out between Arjuna and Duryodhana. Seeing Duryodhana in danger, several other charioteers surrounded Arjuna. In response, Dhanajay repeatedly gave a *tankar* with his bow to signal the Pandavas, and Krishna blew his conch, *Panchajanya*.

Hearing this, Yudhishthira instructed Satyaki to go forward and assist Dhanajay. Satyaki proceeded, entrusting Bhima with Yudhishthira's protection. Drona tried to block Satyaki's path but was defeated, and Satyaki overcame the Kaurava forces, including Dushasana. Later, at Yudhishthira's command, Bhima also headed towards Krishna and Arjuna. Karna engaged Bhima in battle and managed to defeat him. At that moment, Dhanajay attacked Karna, forcing him to retreat. Bhima then boarded Satyaki's chariot and advanced towards Dhanajay.

Bhurishrava attempted to stop Satyaki, but Satyaki killed him. Arjuna then said to Krishna, "The sun is not far from setting. Take the chariot to Jayadratha so that I can fulfil my vow." Seeing Dhanajay approach, Karna, Shalya, Ashwatthama, Duryodhana, and others prepared to fight. Arjuna, fighting fiercely, gradually closed in on Jayadratha. Duryodhana, Karna, Kripa, and others tried to block him. As sunset neared, Krishna used his divine power to cover the sun.

The Kaurava warriors rejoiced, thinking the sun had set and that Arjuna would now enter the fire, having failed his vow. Jayadratha, too, felt relieved and looked up at the sky, free of fear. Just then, Dhanajay rushed towards him. As darkness and dust filled the battlefield, the warriors could no longer see one another. Terrified by Arjuna's arrows, soldiers began fleeing in panic.

At that moment, Dhanajay shot a fierce arrow that severed Jayadratha's head. Several more arrows from Dhanajay carried the severed head to the lap of Jayadratha's father, Vriddhakshatra, who was performing his evening prayers. Startled, the old man stood up in shock. As a result,

Jayadratha's head fell to the ground, and the old man's own head shattered into many pieces.

Then Krishna removed the cover from the sun. The Kauravas realized everything had happened due to Krishna's divine illusion. They began to mourn. Krishna, Arjuna, Bhima, and Satyaki blew their conch shells in triumph. Hearing the sound, Yudhishthira understood that Jayadratha had been slain.

***

"One person has been punished; now, it is the turn of the others. No one will be spared."

Dhananjaya and Vasudeva went out happily.

***

Sujit Chowdhury was the manager of the Elgin Road branch of the State Bank. The workload had been tremendous for the past few days. After the lunch break, he entered the office and saw an envelope with his name written in English on the table. When he inquired outside, he found out that someone had delivered the envelope for him, but no one had noticed the person's identity.

He opened the envelope and found a piece of paper inside, bearing a drawing of a bow and arrow along with the words *DEATH SENTENCE* printed in red ink in English. His heart sank at the sight. He could not concentrate on his work and decided to go back home—it was Saturday, after all. His home was in Tollygunge.

That day, there was an invitation in Garia at the house of a very close relative. He was parking his car there while his wife and daughter had already gone ahead. The place was a bit dark. As he got out of the car, someone said, "You are restless with fear for your life. Remember your old sins. You must receive your punishment." With that, the person left in a hurry. Sujit couldn't see him properly.

What was going on? Was this the same person who had brought the envelope to the office? But why? What was his intention?

"Anyway, I have to move on…" he thought and joined the event, though his mind remained distracted.

He returned home and lay down, but he could not sleep at all. Countless thoughts crowded his mind.

***

The Kauravas, with Karna as their commander, began fighting the Pandavas. At one point during the battle, Duhshasana encountered Bhima. The two attacked each other, and a fierce battle ensued between them.

***

The next morning, while reading the newspaper, Sujit received a call from his elder brother, Bijit Chowdhury, who lived in their ancestral home in Ballygunge with their father, Nrisingha Chowdhury. He sounded worried.

"Baba is not well. Come immediately," he said.

Hearing this, Sujit became anxious. Their father was already unwell—who knew what had happened now? He quickly left for Ballygunge. Since it was Sunday and the roads were relatively empty, he reached in no time. When he arrived, he saw Dr. Banerjee was attending to his father.

"I've given him medicine. Let me know how he is doing later," said Dr. Banerjee.

"There won't be any further issues, right?" Bijit asked.

"I don't think so."

"He suddenly became very restless," Bijit added.

"*Dadan* was watching a serial while taking tea. Suddenly, during a murder scene, he started mumbling," said Pralaya, Bijit's son.

"Nrisingha Babu is very addicted to watching serials," said Bijit.

"Alright, please ask him to avoid any excitement. If there's any issue, call me," Dr. Banerjee said before leaving.

"How are you feeling now?" Sujit asked his father.

"I'm fine. But you all should be a bit careful."

"Why? What will happen to us?"

"I'm so scared... so scared!"

"Stop watching so many serials! That's why you're in this condition!"

Nrisingha Babu was suffering from extreme fear. He was having frequent nightmares and kept recalling incidents from the past. Whenever that happened, he became terrified for the safety of his sons. He loved them deeply and could not bear the thought of anything happening to them.

He had warned them repeatedly. He had overheard their plans earlier. But… they had not listened. He had witnessed everything—helplessly, like a silent spectator.

***

Krishna went to Hastinapur as an envoy of the Pandavas. Upon hearing the news of Krishna's arrival from a messenger, Dhritarashtra was very pleased and instructed Duryodhana to give him a proper reception.

Duryodhana said, "I cannot enjoy the kingdom alongside the Pandavas. I have decided to imprison Krishna—once that is done, the Yadavas, the Pandavas, and the entire world will fall under my control."

Hearing this, Dhritarashtra and Bhishma forbade him from committing such a heinous act. When Krishna arrived in Hastinapur, the Kauravas welcomed him. He first went to Dhritarashtra. After a brief conversation, he visited Vidura's house and later met Kunti. He then went to Duryodhana's palace. After the formal reception, Duryodhana invited him to dine, but Krishna declined and, instead, returned to Vidura's house, where he took his meal. Vidura warned him about Duryodhana's evil intentions. Krishna assured him there was no need to worry—he had come to resolve all problems.

The next morning, Krishna proceeded to the royal court. Dhritarashtra, Bhishma, Drona, and others received him with great respect.

Krishna addressed Dhritarashtra, "I have come here to ensure peace between the Kauravas and the Pandavas so that none are destroyed. Your lineage is among the noblest, and injustice must not stain it. Duryodhana and your other sons are greedy and unruly—they are treating their own kin with hostility. The Kauravas are in grave danger. If you ignore this, everything will be lost. But if you wish, you can still avert this disaster. Discipline your sons and pursue peace, and all will be well. With the Pandavas by your side, even Indra will not be able to conquer you. But ask yourself—will you be happy if either the Pandavas or your sons are killed in war? Protect your innocent subjects as well. The fatherless Pandavas grew up under your care—continue to look after them. Give them their rightful share of the kingdom. This is their humble request. Your Majesty, the Pandavas are willing to serve you, but they are also prepared to fight. Do what you believe is right."

All the kings present silently praised Krishna in their hearts, though none voiced their agreement. Parashurama, Maharshi Kanva, Narada, and others tried to persuade Duryodhana, but their efforts were in vain.

Then Dhritarashtra said, "I, too, desire peace, but I lack the strength. My wicked sons will not obey me. Duryodhana listens to no one. Please, you try to convince him yourself."

Krishna then tried to reason with Duryodhana, urging him to do what was right. All his elders—Dhritarashtra, Bhishma, Drona, Vikarna, Sanjaya, and others—wanted peace. Krishna reminded him that although he had always been hostile to the Pandavas, they had tolerated much. Now, he was enjoying a kingdom the Pandavas had conquered. Even if all his warriors fought together, they would not be able to stand against Arjuna. Therefore, he should ensure that the

Kaurava dynasty is not destroyed. He must give the Pandavas half of the kingdom.

Bhishma, Drona, Vidura, and Dhritarashtra all urged Duryodhana to accept Krishna's proposal, but Duryodhana remained defiant. He said, "I will not give even as much land as can be pierced by the tip of a needle."

Krishna, now angry, smiled and said, "You and your allies will attain *Veerashraya* (a warrior's death)."

Duryodhana left the court with his brothers and companions. Krishna turned to Dhritarashtra and said, "Your Majesty, do not let everything be destroyed because of your weakness. Bind Duryodhana, Duhshasana, Shakuni, and Karna, and hand them over to the Pandavas. Establish peace."

Dhritarashtra then summoned Gandhari and asked her to convince Duryodhana. He was called back. Gandhari pleaded with her son to heed Krishna's words, but instead of listening, Duryodhana became enraged. He consulted with Shakuni, Karna, and Duhshasana and decided to imprison Krishna.

Sensing their intention, Satyaki and Kritavarma prepared themselves. Vidura warned Dhritarashtra, "Your Majesty, your sons are planning something reckless and impossible."

Dhritarashtra again summoned Duryodhana and warned him.

Krishna said, "Duryodhana, you think I am alone—that is why you dare to imprison me." Saying this, he laughed loudly. Suddenly, divine forms began appearing all over his body. His form expanded, displaying thousands of feet and arms, dazzling and armed. Everyone in the assembly was struck with fear.

At their request, Krishna returned to his previous form and walked out, holding the hands of Satyaki and Vidura.

As Krishna was about to board his chariot and leave, Dhritarashtra approached him and said, "You have now seen how little influence I have over my sons. You heard what I said to Duryodhana. I harbour no ill will. Everyone knows I have tried every means to make peace."

Krishna replied to Dhritarashtra, Bhishma, Drona, and the others, "You all witnessed what happened in the Kaurava court. You saw Duryodhana attempt to imprison me. Dhritarashtra himself admitted his powerlessness. I shall now take my leave."

***

Seeing that his father was feeling much better, Sujit left his elder brother's place after chatting for a while and started heading home. Both his body and mind felt exhausted. He decided to stop by the coffee shop for a cup of coffee. He parked his car and had just stepped out when an arrow struck his chest. At that moment, he heard someone say, "Now you die." Everyone saw a person, disguised as a warrior, shoot the arrow and flee.

The people on the street, who witnessed the incident in shock, initially thought it was some kind of *bohurupee* joking. But when Sujit collapsed, they rushed to help. Blood was flowing everywhere. The ambulance and police were immediately informed. However, he died before he could be taken to the ambulance.

The police spoke to eyewitnesses and learned that the two assailants were dressed as warriors. Suddenly, one of them fired the arrow, and the other said something before both fled the scene. No one had noticed anything unusual beforehand. There were no CCTV cameras in the area, so no leads could be found.

The police contacted Sujit's family and informed them about his death. A wave of grief swept over the household. Bijit was stunned upon hearing the news, and Nrisingha Babu collapsed in sorrow.

***

Karna was engaged in battle with the Panchalas. When one of Dhrishtadyumna's sons was killed by his arrow, Krishna urged Arjuna to kill Karna immediately. As Arjuna advanced, Bhima joined him and began protecting him from behind.

At that moment, Duhshasana confronted Bhima, and the two attacked each other fiercely. Bhima's arrow shattered Duhshasana's bow and flag and killed his charioteer. Duhshasana then took control of the chariot himself, picked up another bow, and shot Bhima, rendering him unconscious for a while. As soon as Bhima regained consciousness, Duhshasana attacked again. Enraged, Bhima shouted, "Today, I will drink your blood, you evil spirit!"

Duhshasana hurled a powerful weapon, but Bhima swung his club and smashed it. Bhima's club struck

Duhshasana on the head, sending him flying and destroying his horse and chariot.

Duhshasana writhed in pain. Furious, Bhima leapt down from his chariot and assaulted Duhshasana, pressing his foot against his throat. He then pierced his chest with a sharp spear and drank his blood. After beheading Duhshasana, he began to taste the blood.

The soldiers who witnessed the bloodthirsty Bhima dropped their weapons and fled in fear.

Then Bhima roared, "I vowed to drink Duhshasana's blood, and I have fulfilled that vow. Next, I will kill Duryodhana. Only then will I find peace." Saying this, Bhima let out another mighty roar.

***

"I was desperate to finish him off," said Dhananjaya.

"Are you satisfied now?" Vasudeva asked gently.

"Certainly, now the next target..." Dhananjaya said as his eyes burned with resolve.

***

It was afternoon. Anirban Dasgupta was relaxing with a cup of tea in his hand. He was alone in his private room on the fifth floor, enjoying the view of the sunset. The room had glass walls on three sides, and when the curtains were drawn back, the outside world was clearly visible. Suddenly, his eyes fell on one side of the glass. There was some writing. He approached and saw the words *Death Warrant* written in red ink. Next to it was an arrow, also in red ink.

"What is this?" His heart trembled involuntarily. What an ominous sign! He called the office staff and showed them. No one could explain it. The writing was quickly erased.

His body and mind felt unwell. He returned home early. His residence was in Ballygunge, and he was in the car business.

"In a bad mood? Feeling unwell?" his wife Srabanti asked when she saw him return early.

"No, nothing like that... just feeling a little tired," he replied.

"All the time it's work, work, work! Now take a little rest," she said.

But the incident continued to bother him. Then came his birthday. There were many guests, and at one point, he needed to step out for a while. As he was about to get out of the car, he noticed another message written in red ink in front of him: *After the birthday comes the day of death. Be careful.*

His head started spinning. He did not go out after that. Still, he thought it would be best not to tell anyone. If they knew, they would probably panic. So what was the point? But the real question remained—who was behind all this?

***

Grandfather Bhishma was lying on his deathbed on the *Sharasajya*. Dronacharya had been killed. After that, Duryodhana began discussing the next course of action with all the kings. They advised him to appoint the great warrior

Karna as the chief commander and lead the army. Duryodhana then requested Karna to take up the position. Karna agreed, and Duryodhana, overjoyed, appointed him as the chief commander in a grand ceremony. He felt confident that this time, their victory was certain.

The next day, at sunrise, Karna, adorned in his finest war gear, set out for battle, blowing his conch. Arjuna prepared for the battle by arranging the troops in a formation known as the *crescent moon* (*Chandrakala Vyuha*). War drums echoed on both sides, and the warriors roared like lions. A fierce battle ensued, during which the Kauravas suffered greater losses.

The following morning, Karna vowed to Duryodhana that he would either kill Arjuna or die trying. He requested Shalya to be his charioteer. However, Shalya became furious upon hearing this and initially refused. Yet, unable to go against Duryodhana's wishes, he finally agreed.

Then, as the chariots were readied, another intense battle began.

***

Anirban returned home and sat silently. Was someone threatening him? But why? For money—or something else?

"What are you doing sitting here, Papa? Everyone wants to meet you," his daughter said as she came and called him.

"Yes, yes, let's go..."

There was no flaw in the arrangements. The atmosphere was joyful, but within it, only he lacked peace.

The same thoughts plagued him at night. He didn't even realize when he fell asleep.

When Srabanti woke up in the morning, she saw that Anirban wasn't there. This was normal—it was his habit to wake up early every morning and go out for a jog. So, she assumed he was fine, although he hadn't been feeling well for the last two days.

Suddenly, she heard a scream and rushed out. The maid, Kajal, was shouting, "Come here quickly, everyone! Look at the devastation!"

In the small garden next to the house lay Anirban's lifeless body, an arrow piercing the left side of his chest.

Hearing the screams, everyone in the house came running. Srabanti nearly fainted; someone held her. Everyone was shocked by the suddenness of the incident.

The police arrived a little later, and the interrogation began.

"I've never seen a murder case involving arrows," said Inspector Nishith Samaddar.

"I haven't seen it either," said Sub-Inspector Prabal Dutta.

The body was sent for post-mortem. A shadow of grief fell over the entire house.

***

Karna was fighting with great bravery and wounded Yudhishthira in the battle. Then, Bhima attacked Karna, and due to Bhima's powerful blow, Karna fell unconscious and slumped in his chariot. Shalya quickly took him away from the battlefield. The Kaurava warriors—Duryodhana, Ashwatthama, and others—then came forward to continue the fight.

The sons of Dhritarashtra surrounded Bhima and attacked him from all sides, but Bhima killed many of them. Karna later destroyed Bhima's bow and chariot. Undeterred, Bhima grabbed his club and began killing enemy soldiers with it.

At that time, Arjuna also began decimating the Kaurava army. Duryodhana and his warriors entered the fray, and Ashwatthama fought with great ferocity. Under the force of Ashwatthama's arrows, Yudhishthira was forced to leave the battlefield.

Dhrishtadyumna then began fighting Duryodhana. When Duryodhana's chariot was destroyed, he mounted another and withdrew. Karna then attacked Dhrishtadyumna. Soon, Yudhishthira returned to the battlefield, joined by Nakula, Sahadeva, Satyaki, Draupadi's five sons, Shikhandi, and others, and they all surrounded Karna.

Karna again wounded Yudhishthira, who then retreated with Nakula and Sahadeva to rejoin the main army. Bhima, fulfilling his terrible vow, killed Duhshasana and drank his blood. He then went on to kill ten more sons of Dhritarashtra. Meanwhile, Karna's son, Vrishasena, was slain by Arjuna's arrow.

Grieving for his son, Karna was consumed with rage and challenged Arjuna to a duel. A fierce and devastating battle ensued, with both warriors launching terrifying weapons at each other. Arjuna killed many Kaurava soldiers during the fight.

Karna successfully repelled Arjuna's attacks and struck him with a hundred small arrows. In response, Arjuna fitted a fresh bowstring to *Gandiva* and showered Karna with a barrage of arrows. Seeing this, the Kauravas abandoned Karna and fled. Then Karna released a fearsome arrow that struck Arjuna's chariot. Krishna, realizing the danger, pressed the chariot down with his foot. The impact of the arrow burned Arjuna's crown, causing it to fall off.

Krishna then lifted the sunken chariot with both hands. Arjuna, regaining control, slashed Karna's crown, earrings, and shining armour into pieces with his sword, and in the process, injured him. Karna responded by firing arrows at both Krishna and Arjuna.

At that moment, the wheels of Karna's chariot got stuck in the ground. Even then, Karna continued shooting and repeatedly tried to cut Arjuna's bowstring. On Krishna's advice, Arjuna prepared a terrible divine weapon. Meanwhile, the chariot wheels sank even deeper. Karna shouted, "Let me raise the chariot first; then we will fight. Follow the laws of war!"

Krishna responded, "Now you remember the law of war? When injustice was done to the Pandavas, where was your sense of righteousness? If you didn't remember *dharma* then, there's no meaning in invoking it now. You shall find no mercy."

Enraged, Karna took up his bow and aimed a deadly arrow at Arjuna. The arrow struck Arjuna's arm, dazing him. His head spun, and *Gandiva* slipped from his hand. Seizing the moment, Karna jumped down to lift his stuck chariot wheel—but failed.

Arjuna regained consciousness and drew a powerful arrow called *Anjolik* from his quiver. With it, he severed Karna's head. Krishna, Arjuna, and the other Pandavas rejoiced and blew their conch shells. Their army erupted in celebration, blowing trumpets and roaring with triumph. The Madra king, Shalya, silently left with his chariot without a flag.

***

The conversation before Anirban's death went like this—

"What happened? Do you remember everything this time?"

"What do you want?"

"I want to finish you off."

"If you kill me like this—alone and unarmed—you will be punished by dharma!"

"You are talking about *dharma*? What a joke. Where was your *dharma* that day? You have no right to speak of it."

"Then it's all over."

As Dhananjaya and Vasudeva reflected on these words, they gradually moved away… far away. There was still much left to be done.

***

Surya returned home early in the afternoon. Krishna was also at home.

"We haven't played chess in a long time—let's do it," Surya said.

The two of them sat down with the chessboard. The game of checkmate and counter-checkmate began.

"You've become quite a skilled chess player in just a few days," Krishna remarked.

At that moment, Ujjaini arrived.

"I see the game is quite intense," she said.

"Why don't you join us?" Krishna offered.

"No more playing. Let's go to your roof. It's been a long time," she suggested.

"Okay, let's go," Krishna agreed.

The beautiful sunset seemed to be waiting for them. They started taking pictures.

"Wonderful!" Surya exclaimed.

"It's as if someone skillfully painted a picture on the canvas of the sky with a brush," Ujjaini added.

After a while, Krishna pointed and asked, "Tell me, what flower is this?"

"I can't say. You tell me," Ujjaini replied.

"Azalea."

"Wow, how beautiful. You've really created a wonderful garden," she said.

By then, darkness had fallen, and they came back downstairs.

"I've made a new kind of ice cream. Wait, I'll bring it," Krishna said and went to get it.

After eating the ice cream, Ujjaini said, "Excellent! You must share the recipe with me."

"Of course," Krishna replied.

"Well, have you read in the newspaper about those three people killed in a row—shot with arrows?"

"Yes, I have," Surya said.

"What do you think about the incidents?"

"Nothing, really. I didn't bother much about it. I didn't get the case. The police are investigating."

"It would be good if you got the case," Krishna said.

"Yes, it would be very good," Ujjaini agreed.

***

It turned out that the murderers had strong willpower. The case came to Surya. Two days later, in the morning, Manas Babu's call came on Surya's mobile.

"Yes, Manas da..."

Manas Babu was the big boss of Lalbazar.

"I have been feeling quite unwell for a few days, so I couldn't go to the office. You must have read about the murders by shooting arrows in the newspaper. There have been three murders in a row. There's a lot of fuss about this. Arijit Saha is looking into the case, but he can't quite figure it out. I asked him to seek your help. Arijit might come to you today. I gave him your phone number. I know you can definitely handle it."

"I don't know if I can do it or not, but I will try. I'll do my best to honour your trust."

"Thank you. We'll talk again later."

After a while, Arijit called Surya and said he would come to him in the evening.

"Your wish has been fulfilled," Surya told Krishna.

"Good," Krishna said.

***

Arijit came in the evening.

"I'm familiar with your name. You're very famous in your field, and Manas da praises you a lot," he said while sipping his tea.

"Manas da exaggerated," Surya replied.

"Not at all. There's a lot to learn from you. I also know about Krishna—he's an artist. Now, let's come to the main point. You must have read about the incident in the newspaper?"

"Yes, I have. Still, I'd like to hear everything from you."

"Sure, I'll tell you. I visited the spot in all three cases."

Surya listened carefully, and then said, "I'm thinking of visiting those three places myself."

"Alright, let's go. Just tell me when."

"The day after tomorrow is Sunday. I'll be free then. We can go that day."

"Okay, so be it. I'll come and pick you up at ten in the morning."

"I'll be ready. But Krishna will be with me."

"Of course, he's welcome. But you need to close this case. I haven't made any progress. You're our only hope now. And one more thing—each of the three murders was committed using arrows, as you know. But nothing was stolen in any of the cases."

"That means theft or robbery wasn't the motive. It could be revenge."

"Yes, that's what it seems. Alright, let's go and see."

As Arijit was leaving, Krishna said, "He seems like a pretty decent guy."

"That's true, but I'm really hungry."

"Me too. Let's eat, then."

***

The next morning, they went out with Arijit. Krishna had already told Ujjaini everything.

"You will be successful," Ujjaini said.

First, they went to the house of Ranajoy Sarkar, who had been the first victim.

"Come in, sir," someone greeted them.

"This is Subhankar, Ranajoy Babu's manager," Arijit introduced. "Let's see the place."

Surya carefully examined the spot where Ranajoy Babu's body had been found. He had been shot in the back, suggesting that he might have tried to flee upstairs and lock himself in the room—but he could not escape his death.

"As soon as he started running, the arrow pierced his back," Surya said.

"That's what it looks like," Arijit agreed.

"And the murderer/murderers seems/seem to be quite skilled in targeting. Murders using bows and arrows are almost unheard of these days. From that perspective, this case is rather unusual. Well, I'd like to talk to Subhankar Babu for a bit."

"Yes…" Subhankar looked at him.

"How long have you been working for him?"

"Six months. But during that time, he had become very dependent on me. He had a son, Suman, who lives in Delhi. He came and then left. He'll return in a few days. Ranajoy Babu's wife died a long time ago."

"What do you think about this incident?"

"I don't understand anything. But just before it happened, something strange occurred."

"What happened?"

"When the shop was closing at night, someone threw a stone and broke the shop's window. But no one was seen. I wasn't in the shop at the time. Sunil informed me."

"Who is Sunil?"

"The security guard of our shop."

"Okay, I need to talk to him. I'll also need to speak to Suman Babu. Please give me his mobile number."

Subhankar gave Suman's mobile number to Surya.

"I checked the shop's CCTV footage but couldn't make out anything. I'll show it to you," Arijit said.

"Alright, I'll take a look," Surya replied. "Now, Subhankar Babu, think carefully. Did anyone have any enmity with him?"

"No, there wasn't anything like that. But yes—Montu once threatened him."

"Who is Montu?"

"A local hooligan. There was going to be a *jalsa* in the neighbourhood, and he asked for a donation of five thousand rupees. But Ranajoy Babu refused to give money for such activities, so Montu threatened him."

"You didn't mention that before," Arijit said.

"I couldn't remember it earlier, sir, but now I do."

"That could be," Surya said. "We need to bring Montu in for interrogation. But I don't think he'd kill him for such a small issue. Still, wherever you see ashes, blow them up and see..."

"You might find a priceless gem," Krishna said. After a long silence, he finally got a chance to speak.

"Wow, what a worthy assistant!" Arijit chuckled, and then added, "Alright, I'll make arrangements to pick up Montu."

"Okay, there's nothing more to see here. Let's go to the store. We need to speak with Sunil as well. One more thing—does this house have a CCTV camera?"

"No, not at all," Subhankar replied.

Surya visited the shop and spoke to Sunil.

"Their shop is open even on Sundays, you know!" Krishna remarked.

"Many shops are open on Sundays. Do you find that significant?"

"Let's think about it. You must have understood the real point."

"No, not really. Let's move on to the next place."

***

Then they went to Tollygunge, to Sujit Chowdhury's house. Sujit's wife and daughter had expressions of grief on their faces. They could not say anything; they had no idea whether he had any enemies.

As they were leaving the house, Krishna said, "Now, let's go to the place where he was murdered."

"No, it's no use going there," Surya said to Krishna. "I'll go to his office tomorrow instead. I have to talk to his father and grandfather too."

Next, they went to the house of the third victim, Anirban Dasgupta.

"I know this is not the right time, but I would ask you a few questions for the sake of the investigation; please cooperate with us," Surya said to Srabanti, Anirban's wife.

"No, no, I don't mind. I also want the person—or people—who took my husband's life so brutally to be severely punished."

"We want that too. Well, did anyone in the house hear any sound at that time?"

"No. We were all asleep. Actually, it was his habit to go out jogging early in the morning. That day was no different."

"Did you notice any changes in his behaviour in the past few days?"

"Yes, he seemed quite restless after returning from the office the day before. But when I asked, he didn't say anything."

"Can you guess what might have been troubling him?"

"No, I can't think of anything. We don't have any enemies."

"Okay, I won't bother you anymore."

Then they went to the murder site—the garden.

"You see, there are a lot of big trees here," Krishna said.

"Maybe that's why the murderer—or murderers—had an advantage. The visibility from outside was limited. And maybe no one heard the victim's cries," Surya said.

"Let's see the exact spot. The body was lying face down," Arijit said.

"That means the arrows were fired from the front," Surya observed.

"That's right. No one nearby saw or heard anything. After all, it was early morning."

Surya examined the place thoroughly. Then he said, "There's nothing more to see here. Let's go."

"Okay, I'm in a hurry, too; we'll talk later," said Arijit, and with that, he said goodbye.

***

"I'm really hungry," Krishna said as they were heading home.

"Okay, let's go to a restaurant."

While they were leaving the restaurant after eating, Ujjaini's call came on Surya's mobile.

"Where are you now?" she asked.

"I'm out on an investigation."

"Oh, very good. Come to our house in the afternoon. You're invited today."

"On what occasion?"

"There's no particular occasion. *Baba* just said you should come today."

"Okay, okay, I'll come."

Hearing this, Krishna said, "That's great! After a long time, we'll get to eat *nemontonno*."

The evening went well.

"How is the investigation going?" Ujjaini asked eagerly.

"There hasn't been much progress yet," Surya replied.

"Don't worry. The solution will come in a few days."

"Surya da is the best detective in the world," Krishna added.

"Now, now, here comes the one…" Surya said.

***

The next evening, Krishna said, "Really, in this day and age, it's strange to murder someone with arrows. Isn't it, Surya da?"

"Maybe the killer—or killers—wants to send some kind of message through this," Surya said thoughtfully.

"That could be the reason too…"

"Do you know anything about the history of the bow and arrow?"

"No, please tell me."

"The use of bows and arrows dates back a long time. Archery has been used in warfare, hunting, and even as a sport. The oldest arrow marks were discovered in the Sibudu Caves of South Africa, where arrowheads about sixty to seventy thousand years old have been found—some of which were probably poisoned. In addition, bows and arrows or their traces have been found in many other parts of the world. The Vedas mention the use of bows and arrows. Similarly, the stories in the *Ramayana* and the *Mahabharata* also describe battles involving them."

"Ramachandra broke Lord Shiva's bow, and Arjuna hit the target in Draupadi's *swayamvar,*" Krishna added.

"Yes, exactly. There's even a cave painting in Bhimbetka, Madhya Pradesh, that depicts hunting with bows and arrows."

"We've seen the diary of that caveman, haven't we?"

"Bows and arrows were mainly made of wood, metal, and stone. In some cases, poison was applied to the arrowheads. Various tribes used them extensively. However, with the advent of guns and cannons, their use began to decline. Archery also evolved into a sport and is now part of the Olympic Games. Our own Limba Ram, Dola Banerjee, and Rahul Banerjee are renowned archers. Still, it's hard to imagine that in today's modern metropolis, people are being murdered one after another with bows and arrows."

"Your way of speaking is quite elegant, too."

"Thank you. Let's see how far we can go."

***

Surya visited several places to gather information, including Nrisingha Babu's house and Anirban's office. However, he could not find any specific leads.

It wasn't particularly difficult to catch Montu, but interrogating him proved to be of no use.

"It seems Montu is not involved in this matter," Arijit told Surya over the phone. "He was in the hospital at the time of the murder. His father is admitted there. I've inquired, and many people have confirmed it. Have you found any clue?"

"Not yet. Tell me one thing—was any poison found on the arrows that pierced the bodies of the three victims?"

"No, I have carefully read the post-mortem reports of all three."

"Okay. Can I also see those reports?"

"Of course. I'll arrange it."

"Thank you. We'll talk again later. All the best."

***

Later, Surya also checked the post-mortem reports of the three victims.

In the evening, while Surya was reflecting on the three murders, some new thoughts suddenly came to his mind.

"Are you thinking about the Saraghat mystery?" Krishna asked as he approached.

"Yes, the term is fantastic—*the Saraghat mystery*. Well, something has to be done."

"It will be done," Krishna replied.

***

Shamik Datta Ray was a well-known political leader. On that particular day, he was in Barasat for an election campaign. It had been a hectic and exhausting day, and after the long hours of campaigning, he was finally resting. Just then, the food arrived. One plate contained fried rice. But when he opened the other plate, he was stunned—inside were blood-stained chicken feathers.

Furious, he immediately flung the plate aside and called for his aides. Everyone was shocked. How could such a thing have happened?

"Something has gone wrong, sir. I'll arrange fresh food immediately," said Alok, his trusted companion.

A new plate of fried rice and chicken curry arrived shortly after. But the mystery remained—no one knew how or why the earlier incident had occurred.

Since it was not a particularly serious matter, Shamik chose not to create a scene. Speaking out might have seemed petty, even absurd, so he kept silent. Yet, the incident lingered in his mind.

Upon returning home to his palatial mansion in Salt Lake, he went straight to his room. Everyone in the house was familiar with his habits and respected his privacy, so no one questioned him.

Was this an ominous sign? He wondered.

***

Upon receiving the invitation from the Pandavas, King Shalya of Madra set out to join them, accompanied by his sons and army. Hearing of his journey, Duryodhana organized a lavish reception for him along the way. Shalya was honoured by Duryodhana's attendants and felt pleased by the warm welcome. Grateful for the gesture, he said to Duryodhana, "Tell me your desire."

As the brother of Madri—the mother of Nakula and Sahadeva—Shalya was the maternal uncle of the Pandavas. However, when Duryodhana requested that he join the

Kaurava side in the upcoming war, Shalya agreed to his request.

Later, Shalya went to meet Yudhishthira at the Pandava camp. After greeting the Pandavas, he informed Yudhishthira of the promise he had made to Duryodhana. Yudhishthira responded, "Very well, but you must do something for our benefit. During the war, you will serve as Karna's charioteer. Undermine his confidence and help protect Arjuna."

Shalya assured him, saying, "I will certainly do that. Do not worry—you will emerge victorious." Pleased by his words, Yudhishthira thanked him, and Shalya took leave of the Pandavas to return to the Kaurava camp.

Following the fall of Bhishma and Dronacharya in the Kurukshetra war, the Kauravas appointed Karna as their new commander. However, their defeats continued. Karna then requested Duryodhana to assign Shalya as his charioteer. Though Shalya initially refused, Duryodhana eventually persuaded him with kind words, and Shalya agreed to take on the role.

***

Soon, Shamik had to attend an important meeting. He didn't feel like going, but he had no choice. After the meeting, just as he was about to get into his car, he noticed a piece of paper stuck to the car's window. Written on it in red ink were the chilling words: *"It's time to be punished for your sins. Get ready to die."*

His hands and feet began to tremble. He picked up the note, crumpled it, threw it away, and quickly got into the car.

The driver said he hadn't seen anything. Shamik didn't say much to him either. But the questions kept haunting him—who was behind this? And why? Was it someone from the opposition? Or perhaps an old enemy?

He returned home with a deep, unspoken fear lodged in his heart.

***

When Karna was killed in a fierce battle with Arjuna, Shalya brought the tragic news to Duryodhana. Upon hearing it, Duryodhana was deeply grieved. Following Ashwatthama's advice, he appointed Shalya as the new commander-in-chief.

The Kaurava army, reinvigorated by this decision, let out a mighty roar of encouragement. Shalya then formed a *byuha* called *Sarvatobhadra* and attacked the Pandava army. A brutal and intense battle erupted between the two sides.

***

After returning home, Shamik had some food, took a sleeping pill, and went to bed. The next morning, he woke up feeling much better. He had to travel to Bishnupur, Bankura, for a party campaign. He decided there was no need to tell anyone about what had happened the previous day.

As the day progressed, he became engrossed in work and forgot all about it. After finishing the day's engagements, he found some free time in the evening and went to his bungalow in the Joypur jungle. The atmosphere there was calm and soothing—it felt good to be in such peace.

Suddenly, he heard a noise outside. He stepped out, but no one was there. As he looked around, something sharp suddenly pierced his chest. As he collapsed to the ground, he heard a voice say, *"Even as an uncle, you were part of the worst injustice done to us. Now suffer the punishment."*

Hearing his screams, people came running. But within moments, it was all over. Everyone was in shock. The police were informed.

***

Karna's sons—Chitrasena, Satyasena, and Susharma—were slain by Nakula. Meanwhile, Shalya caused massive destruction to the Pandava army. However, his son was killed by Sahadeva. Shalya then engaged in a fierce battle with Bhima, during which both warriors were seriously injured by each other's blows.

Resuming the fight alongside the Kaurava forces, Shalya continued his assault. At that point, Yudhishthira took a solemn vow to kill him. A fierce duel erupted between Yudhishthira and Shalya. Ultimately, Yudhishthira hurled a devastating weapon that pierced Shalya's chest and Shalya collapsed to the ground.

Yudhishthira also killed Shalya's brother, further demoralizing the Kaurava army, which began to flee in despair. The victorious Pandavas began to shout in joy.

***

"One by one, all the sinners are being eliminated."

"It feels like there's a bit of peace now, but the work isn't over yet."

"It will be completed smoothly, just like this. Come on, let's go."

Dhanajay and Vasudeva said to each other.

***

The phone rang at seven in the morning, and Surya picked it up. It was Manas da calling.

"Good morning, Manas da. How are you?"

"There's nothing much to say about the situation... Have you seen today's newspaper?"

"No... Why? What happened?"

"Another murder with an arrow. The victim was a prominent political leader, so there's quite a commotion."

"Again! When did this happen?"

"Last evening. Can you come to my place this evening?"

"Of course I will."

"Great. I've also asked Arijit to come. We can sit and discuss the matter for a while. And yes, bring Krishna along too."

"Alright."

Surya opened the newspaper and saw that the murder had been given major coverage. It also mentioned the police's failure and reported that the case had now been handed over to him.

Krishna saw the news as well.

"Your name is in it too." he exclaimed.

"Who knows how they get such information," Surya replied.

"Well, the case has been assigned to a well-known person like you, so naturally, it made the news."

"What else can we expect? Murders are happening left and right."

***

At seven in the evening, Surya and Krishna arrived at Manas Babu's residence in Shobhabazar.

"Come in, come in. I was waiting for you," Manas Babu greeted them.

"So, it's another murder," Krishna said.

"Don't say anything. I'm going out of my mind. And the media is making it worse," Manas Babu replied.

"Another death in the same manner," Surya said. "Did you hear anything from those who were with the victim?"

"No, nothing at all. They couldn't say anything. What do you think?"

"I suspect it's someone seeking revenge. Another possibility is that a maniac is behind this. It could be a serial killer."

"But can someone like that plan and execute so many murders? And no clues have been found in any of the cases."

"It's possible. If you look into criminal history, you'll find such patterns. Besides, there are signs that more than one person might be involved."

"That could be. But how will this ever be solved?"

"It seems there is a solution…" Just as Surya was speaking, Arijit walked in. Everyone turned to look at him.

Sitting on the sofa, Arijit said, "I reached that bungalow in the Joypur Forest after receiving the news. There, I saw a half-crazed man muttering, 'Die, die. One by one, all will die.' I asked him, 'Was it because of the arrow?' He smiled and said, 'That must be it,' and then suddenly started running. I chased him down and caught him. But despite repeated questioning, I couldn't get much out of him. I've locked him up for now."

"How are you so sure he's connected to all this?" Krishna asked.

"I believe he is. I'll interrogate him properly tomorrow. Surya Babu, I'll need you there."

"Alright, I'll come," Surya replied.

"That's good," said Manas Babu. "Now, everyone, please have some tea. Krishna, you always surprise me with your cooking—try the fish fry here."

"How's your health now?" Surya asked.

"I'm fine. I'll join you tomorrow."

After a while, they got up to leave.

As they stepped out, Krishna said, "This man isn't the real murderer. But you will catch the one who is."

"I believe that," Surya said. "You certainly have a gift for intuition."

"Whatever he says," Krishna smiled, "what I say will come true."

***

The next day, Surya and Krishna went to meet the man. Arijit was already interrogating him, with Manas Babu present. The man appeared to be middle-aged, with a stubbled beard, dressed in dirty clothes, and occasionally bursting into laughter.

The interrogation proved fruitless—no useful information could be obtained. A look of disappointment lingered in Arijit's eyes.

Just then, an officer approached and said, "Sir, his name is Vikas. He is highly educated but reportedly lost his mental stability after suddenly losing his job. Everyone around here knows him."

"Time and tide wait for no one…" Vikas murmured.

Krishna and Surya exchanged glances.

"We'll leave now, Manas da. I'll talk to you later," said Surya.

"Alright," Manas Babu replied.

"I told you earlier, didn't I?" Krishna remarked as they stepped outside.

"…But we still have to catch the real murderer," Surya said thoughtfully. "I'm taking a few days off. I need to wander around a bit—but alone."

***

That morning, Surya said, "I'm going away for a couple of days."

"Where are you going?" Krishna asked.

"I'll explain everything later. Please don't be upset."

"Alright," Krishna replied.

Meanwhile, Arijit called once.

***

"The circle is slowly closing in," Dhananjaya said.

"Yes," Vasudeva, his accomplice, replied. "This time, we have to proceed very carefully."

"That's true. But they haven't figured anything out yet."

"Still, there's no harm in staying cautious. Detective Surya has begun the investigation."

"We will reach our goal," they assured each other.

***

Animesh Dasgupta heard a rustling sound. He looked around but saw nothing. Shrugging it off, he returned to his book—a light Bengali short story collection. Lately, he had developed a fondness for such readings. For the past few days, however, a sense of melancholy had enveloped him. Once a renowned advocate, Animesh had owned a large house in New Town and was widely respected. But now, he had stepped away from it all. He spent most of his time reading books.

It was barely nine o'clock at night. He was alone at home; the rest of the family had gone to a relative's house for an invitation. Dinner was already prepared; he planned to have it soon.

Suddenly, a strange voice pierced the silence: "Your days are coming to an end. You will have to face punishment for the terrible sin you have committed."

"What punishment? What sin? Who are you talking about?" he shouted, startled.

No one answered.

"Come forward!" he called out again.

There was still no response. Only a terrifying, echoing laughter filled the house and then, a heavy, oppressive silence settled in.

Animesh sat frozen, panic rising within him. He considered calling his son but changed his mind; he did not want to create any panic in his family. He searched the house thoroughly, upstairs and down. But there was no one. The doors were locked.

Then what was it?

Was it a figment of his imagination? Whose sin had the voice spoken of? His mind was now filled with fear and tension.

***

The king of Gandhara, Shakuni, and his son Uluka were fiercely battling the Pandavas. This was the same Shakuni who, with his cunning strategies, defeated Yudhishthira in a game of dice and caused the Pandavas to lose everything. He was cherished by Duryodhana and his allies but was disliked by many others due to his cunning nature. With valiant warriors like Bhishma, Drona, Karna, and Shalya now gone, the Kauravas stood on the brink of defeat.

***

Animesh's trance was broken by the sound of the doorbell. He quickly got up and opened the door.

"What's wrong with you? Why do you look like that?" his wife, Suparna, asked.

"Nothing happened," he replied, sitting down on the sofa.

"Have you eaten anything?"

"No."

"Are you feeling unwell?"

"I told you, nothing happened," Animesh said, trying to brush it off.

He did not share anything with anyone, but that night, he could not sleep well. The next morning, he woke up wondering if everything had just been a nightmare. Maybe it was. He told himself he needed to erase it all from his mind.

Two days passed, and Animesh seemed to return to normal. The memory of the incident had mostly faded.

That afternoon, just after waking from a nap, he was scrolling through his phone when a WhatsApp message popped up: **"Your death is imminent,"** with bloodstains surrounding the text. The message had come from his son Shaunak's phone.

"What happened now?" his wife exclaimed when she saw his face. Animesh silently showed her the message.

"What is this? Who sent it?"

"Your son," he replied.

"I'm calling him right away."

When Shaunak heard everything, he was stunned.

"I would never send something like that!" he insisted.

"You'd better come quickly. Your father is very disturbed."

Shaunak, an engineer, could not understand how such a message had been sent from his phone. Then he remembered—he had briefly left his room with his phone on the table. But who could have accessed it? And why?

He came home, deeply worried. When he arrived, Animesh finally opened up and told him everything about what he had experienced that night.

"So that's why your face and eyes looked so strange that day," Suparna said.

"Is someone playing mind games with us?" asked Anjali, Shaunak's wife.

"It's possible," Suparna replied.

"Or maybe someone's idea of a joke," Shaunak said.

"But who would play such a cruel joke?" Anjali asked.

Animesh sat silently, still as a stone.

"Your father is truly frightened," Suparna said softly.

"Let's do something," Shaunak suggested. "He needs a change of environment. Take him to Puri for a few days. It will help him recover and forget all this."

"That's a great idea," Anjali agreed.

"Alright, I'll make the arrangements," Shaunak said.

And so it was decided. Shaunak arranged the trip to Puri. After arriving there, Animesh began to feel more like himself. Suparna was happy, too. The calm and vibrant atmosphere of the beach lifted their spirits.

***

Puri is a renowned destination in Odisha. Tourists from various places come here to experience its serene beaches and famous temples. For Bengalis, Puri is almost like a second home. The sea holds an indescribable charm—an invisible pull that draws them back time and again.

The hotel where they were staying was located very close to the sea. From their room window, they could see the vast expanse of the sea.

"We've come here after such a long time," Suparna said.

"It must have been fifteen years," Animesh replied.

They visited Nandankanan, Udayagiri, Khandagiri, the Lingaraja Temple, and the Konark Temple and even spent a day at Chilika Lake. Somewhere along the journey, the fear that had once gripped their minds quietly faded away.

It was eight o'clock at night. They had just returned from the beach and were now sitting in their hotel room, watching television. Dinner would be served a little later. Their son, Shaunak, called them every day to check in.

Suddenly, Animesh's phone rang. He answered, "Okay, I'm coming…"

"What happened?" Suparna asked.

"Someone's calling me downstairs," he replied.

"Who would be calling at this hour?"

"I don't know. He just said we need to talk. Let's see what it's about. Anyway, it'll be good to stretch my legs a bit."

"Alright. Come back soon."

Animesh stepped outside.

Suparna continued watching TV. The serial she was watching was quite intense.

***

"Now, I suppose you remember all those old deeds—your despicable plot?"

"What do you want after all this time?"

"I want revenge. I want to see you destroyed. Then the others—one by one. Prepare to die."

A swift, precise shot and the arrow pierced the left side of the chest. There was a faint cry and then silence. It was all over.

***

Shakuni and his son Uluka were engaged in a fierce battle. Sahadeva killed Uluka with a powerful thrust of his spear. Enraged and overwhelmed with grief, Shakuni continued to fight furiously. He hurled a mighty weapon at Sahadeva, but Sahadeva shattered it mid-air with a powerful arrow and then beheaded Shakuni with a swift strike of his spear. Shakuni's followers were killed by Arjuna.

***

Suparna grew increasingly worried when Animesh did not return even after an hour. Attempts to reach him by phone were unsuccessful. Anxious, she came downstairs.

Manager Ramesh Babu tried to reassure her, saying, "He might have gone somewhere nearby. Let's wait a little longer."

Another half hour passed, but there was still no response despite repeated calls. People searched the surrounding area for Animesh, but their efforts were in vain.

"It's better to inform the police," Ramesh finally said.

Suparna sat in silence, deeply troubled.

***

Dhananjaya and Vasudeva walked slowly along the beach and dropped Animesh's mobile phone into the sea. A sense of satisfaction settled over them, though they knew there was still more work to be done.

***

The phone rang at the police station. A constable answered it and then turned to Inspector Shatapathi to inform him, "Sir, someone just called and said there's an abandoned house not too far from here. He claimed that if we go there, we'll find a body. Then he hung up."

"Did he say anything about himself?" asked Shatapathi.

"No, sir. He didn't. I tried calling the number back, but it couldn't be reached."

"Let's go and check out that house," said Inspector Shatapathi.

Years ago, people used to live in that house, but one day, everyone inside died under mysterious circumstances. Though the police investigated, the case remained unsolved. Since then, the house has been deserted and has earned a reputation for being haunted.

As they were about to leave the police station, Ramesh came rushing in.

"Sir, an elderly man has gone missing from our hotel."

"Alright. Please wait a while—I'll meet you after I finish this task," said Inspector Shatapathi before heading out.

Upon reaching the house, Shatapathi lit his torch and stepped inside. The main door was ajar.

"Sir, look over there…" said a constable.

A mutilated body lay on the floor, surrounded by a pool of blood.

"What a horrific crime," muttered Shatapathi.

After taking photographs, the body was sent for post-mortem. When Shatapathi returned to the police station, he saw Ramesh still waiting.

"Show me the picture of the missing person," he said.

Ramesh had earlier taken a photo of the man, Animesh, along with his wife, Suparna, on his mobile. He showed it to the inspector.

"Who is this woman? His wife?" asked Shatapathi, pointing at Suparna.

"Yes, sir."

Shatapathi compared the photo with the image of the deceased.

"Yes, that's him. He's the man who was killed."

"What did you say? This is terrible!" Ramesh exclaimed in shock.

"Yes. We found his body just a little while ago, pierced by an arrow, in that abandoned house, based on an anonymous phone call."

"What will happen now? This is a disaster!" Ramesh looked completely shaken.

"We need to speak with his wife. Let's go to your hotel," said Shatapathi.

"Alright, sir. Let's go."

***

Suparna was devastated after hearing the news. It was Ramesh who had called Shaunak using his own phone to deliver the terrible update. Shaunak, too, was stunned. He said he would come as soon as possible.

A dark cloud of sorrow descended over the once cheerful atmosphere. Whose cruel hand had taken an innocent life? Was this just the beginning of something more sinister? Inspector Shatapathi was deeply concerned—such an incident had not occurred in recent times. Now, it remained to be seen how the investigation would unfold.

For Dhananjaya and Vasudeva, the past came rushing back—memories of old betrayals, deep injustices, and a secret murder haunted their thoughts. The time for vengeance had finally arrived. Only the real culprit remained.

The news of an advocate being murdered in Puri caused a fresh wave of shock. Arijit immediately travelled to Puri to begin his own investigation.

Meanwhile, Manas Babu called Krishna.

"I can't get through to your *dada*, Surya. What's going on?"

"I can't reach him either. He's gone away for a few days."

"He's hiding. And now, someone else has been killed—this time by a gunshot. Tell him to call me the moment he returns."

"Alright. I'll let him know."

***

Shaunak arrived in Puri very early. On one hand, he had to look after his mother; on the other, he needed to speak with the police. After the post-mortem was completed, he returned to Kolkata with his mother and performed his father's last rites.

Arijit spoke with both Shaunak and Suparna. Suparna explained how Animesh had been living in fear for several days. She also mentioned the disturbing message that had been sent to Animesh's phone from Shaunak's number. When questioned about it, Shaunak said he had no idea how that could have happened. "Why would I, as his son, send such a message to my own father?" he asked, clearly puzzled.

"Alright. I'll speak to you later," Arijit said before leaving. He was deeply concerned.

***

Suddenly, Nrisingha recalled a very old story—a grave injustice that had once taken place. He had warned them many times, but no one had listened. One of his sons had been murdered. The memory made him restless. A low, incoherent mumbling came out of his lips. Alarmed, everyone rushed to him, and he was immediately taken to the hospital.

***

While Dhritarashtra sat alone, mourning and reflecting on the misdeeds of his sons, the sage Vyasa approached him and said, "Maharaj, the time has come for the death of your sons and their companions. Do not grieve. Many lives will be lost in this war, but ultimately, righteousness will prevail. You still have the power to stop this conflict. Do not let your relatives perish. What joy will a kingdom bring you under such circumstances? Let the Pandavas reclaim their rightful share, and let peace return to the Kauravas."

Dhritarashtra replied, "I understand everything, but I am only a human being. I do not wish for injustice to prevail, but you know my sons do not listen to me."

Vyasa then said, "O Maharaj, victory attained through discipline and charity is the highest form. Victory gained through stubbornness is mediocre, and victory achieved solely through war is unjust. A large army does not always guarantee success."

Pointing to Sanjaya, Vyasa added, "I am empowering Sanjaya with *Divyadristi*. He will keep you informed of every detail of the war."

***

"Good morning, Manas da…"

The next morning, a call came to Manas Babu's mobile.

"Hey, Surya! Where have you been? I've been trying to reach you for a long time. Did you look into the case?"

"I just stepped out for a bit…"

"Oh, don't give me excuses. Listen, there's been another murder — just like the previous one. You need to act fast."

"Yes, I'm trying my best."

"Alright, we'll talk again later."

***

Arijit arrived at Surya's house shortly after.

"I heard you've returned. How far did you get?" Arijit asked.

"Not very far. I heard another person has been murdered," said Surya.

"Yes, he was also shot with an arrow," Arijit confirmed.

"Can you tell me the whole story?" Surya asked.

"Of course," Arijit replied, and after narrating the incident, he added, "But I suspect his son. For some reason, he might have wanted his father dead—possibly a property dispute."

"Yes, that's quite possible," Surya agreed.

"So, I'm planning to interrogate him thoroughly," said Arijit.

As Arijit was about to leave, Krishna said, "You seem to be following a lead."

"Maybe," Arijit replied.

"Still, Animesh Babu's son doesn't seem guilty," Krishna remarked.

"Even so, Arijit will arrest him," said Surya.

And that's exactly what happened. The police took Shaunak into custody.

***

Nrisingha Babu's condition had stabilized, and he was scheduled to be discharged from the hospital the next day. He called Bijit and said, "You have to be very careful."

"Why? What's going to happen to me now?" Bijit asked.

"Sujit met a terrible fate… now it's your turn." He held his son's hand, tears welling up in his eyes.

"Forget all that. If you keep thinking about it, you'll fall ill again," Bijit said, trying to comfort him.

Around noon, the cabin was empty, and Nrisingha was dozing lightly. Suddenly, someone shook him awake.

"Are you sleeping or not?"

"Who…?" Nrisingha asked, startled.

"Someone very close to you. You and your sons have caused us immense harm. Even though you knew everything, you didn't try to stop them. You will now face the consequences. We have already destroyed one of your sons, and now the other will die. The rest of the sinners have also been dealt with, one by one. You will come to know everything—and you will burn in grief over your son. That is your punishment."

"No, no, no…!" Nrisingha screamed in horror.

The stranger disappeared.

A nurse came running in after hearing the commotion.

"What happened?" she asked.

"He was here…"

"Who? Who was here?"

"The assassin. The death warrant has been issued."

"I don't understand a word you're saying."

Soon after, Bijit arrived, having been informed of the incident.

"What happened now?" he asked.

Nrisingha recounted the entire episode.

"What are you saying? You must have been dreaming."

"No, it wasn't a dream. It was a terrifying reality. I want to go home—right now."

That very day, Nrisingha returned home. The police were notified. In the evening, Manas Babu called Surya.

"Have you heard any news?"

"No. What news are you talking about?"

"Nrisingha Babu, Sujit's father, was in the hospital. Someone entered his cabin and claimed responsibility for Sujit's murder. He also threatened to kill Bijit and said others had already been eliminated."

"Did anyone else see him?"

"No. There's no CCTV inside the cabin, only one outside. It captured a man entering the cabin and leaving shortly after. He was dressed like hospital staff, wore glasses, and had a beard."

"That sounds like a disguise."

"Exactly. No one recognized him as part of the staff. Arijit questioned everyone."

"I want to meet Nrisingha Babu."

"All right, you can go. I'll inform them."

"Thank you."

***

The next afternoon, Surya went to Nrisingha Babu's house to meet him.

"Did you see him clearly?" he asked.

"Yes, absolutely. He clearly said he was finishing everyone off, one by one. Please... please save my son," Nrisingha Babu pleaded.

"We will definitely protect him. Don't worry," Surya assured him.

He then spoke to Bijit.

"Do you have any enemies?"

"No," Bijit replied.

"Did anything happen in the past that might be relevant?"

"I can't recall anything like that."

"Alright, your security will be arranged. Let's go now."

Surya stood up without waiting any longer. There was nothing more to learn here, so he stepped outside.

The situation was slowly becoming clearer. It seemed increasingly likely that revenge was the motive. Bijit could be the final target. Yet, Surya felt that either Bijit or Nrisingha Babu was hiding something rooted in a past incident.

Somewhere, another arrow was waiting for its last victim.

***

Bijit walked toward his office, where he managed his furniture business. Just as he was about to enter, a toy arrow struck his right foot. It was not clear who had shot it, nor did he feel it necessary to investigate.

He hurried inside, and it did not take long for him to sense that this was a warning—an ominous sign of approaching danger.

His manager, Palash, was sharp and intelligent. Bijit informed him that he would be going on vacation to take some time off and asked him to make all the necessary arrangements and book a chartered flight. He was gripped by a deep fear of death.

***

The Kaurava army gradually grew weaker and more disheartened. Duryodhana tried to boost their morale, and for a while, they resumed fighting with renewed enthusiasm. However, the Pandava army's fierce assault ultimately wiped them out. Duryodhana's eleven Akshauhini armies were completely destroyed.

When Duryodhana realized that no one was left to support him, he left the battlefield alone, clutching his mace. Meanwhile, Sanjaya—who had been reporting the events of the Kurukshetra war to King Dhritarashtra—was captured. However, at Vyasa's request, his life was spared, and he was released.

As Sanjaya made his way away from the battlefield, he encountered a wounded and devastated Duryodhana, still holding his mace. Sanjaya informed him about his brief captivity and release. Duryodhana anxiously asked about his brothers and the fate of his army. Sanjaya replied, "All your brothers have been killed, and your army has been completely annihilated. Only three warriors remain—Kripacharya, Ashwatthama, and Kritavarma."

Duryodhana sighed deeply and said, "Sanjaya, tell King Dhritarashtra that his son Duryodhana has taken refuge in Lake Dwaipayana. All my people have perished. I have no desire to live in this condition. I have abandoned this great war and now lie in the lake, grievously wounded."

With these words, Duryodhana entered the Dwaipayana Lake and, using his illusion, rendered its waters motionless.

Soon after, Ashwatthama, Kripacharya, and Kritavarma arrived at the lake in a chariot. Sanjaya told them everything. After mourning for a while, they departed. Upon receiving the news, a shadow of sorrow fell over the entire Kaurava camp.

***

Arijit arrived in the morning.

"Did I interrupt the tea party?" he asked.

"Oh no, no, *dada*! Just wait — tea and egg toast will be served shortly," Krishna replied.

"Then tell me the news," said Surya.

"Bijit Babu has run away. He didn't even inform his family where he was going. He left his mobile behind and said he would contact them later. He took his passport and some other documents with him."

"As I suspected. But I'm not sure how long he can stay safe after running away. It seems he took a flight. If you search, you'll probably find him."

"Alright, I'll look into it."

As he was leaving after tea and breakfast, Arijit said, "Thank you, Krishna. The breakfast was excellent — especially, the *sandesh*."

***

Two hours later, Arijit called. "I searched as you asked and got the news—he has gone to Hyderabad."

"Then we should go too. Otherwise, it will be difficult to save him. They must have already got the news that he is in Hyderabad," said Surya.

"But how will you find him in such a big city?" Arijit asked.

"We'll go and see. If nothing else, we'll just have to roam around. And our Krishna loves to travel," Surya replied.

"Okay, I'll call you later," said Arijit, and then hung up.

"We're going to Hyderabad, then," said Krishna.

"Yes. Are you happy?" asked Surya.

"Of course! We'll visit Charminar, Film City, Salar Jung Museum, Nizam Palace…" Krishna began enthusiastically.

"But we're going there for work. And it's a serious job—we have to save someone," Surya interrupted.

"We'll work, and we'll travel too. Whatever case Detective Surya Chatterjee takes on, he always cracks it," Krishna joked.

"Enough of that! Now go pack your bags!" Surya said sternly.

A little later, Ujjaini called Surya to check in.

"So, the mission is now Hyderabad," she said.

"Let's see what happens," Surya replied.

"All the best," said Ujjaini.

After Surya hung up, Krishna turned to him and said, "So our main task now is to save Bijit Babu."

"Not just that—we have to find the murderer or murderers, too," Surya added.

"Exactly," Krishna agreed.

"And once everything is sorted, we can go sightseeing," Krishna said with a grin.

"That's a promise," Surya replied with a smile.

***

"The bird has escaped," Dhananjaya said.

"Where can it escape to? I know where he has gone," Vasudeva replied.

"Where has he gone?" Dhananjaya asked anxiously.

"Hyderabad,' Vasudeva answered.

"Alright, then that's where our path of revenge ends," Dhananjaya said.

***

The Pandavas searched for a long time but were unable to find Duryodhana anywhere. Eventually, exhausted, they returned to their camp. Meanwhile, Kripacharya, Ashwatthama, and Kritavarma went to Dwaipayana Lake and called out, "O King, rise! Let us join forces and fight the Pandavas together. Either emerge victorious or attain heroic glory."

Duryodhana replied, "I am wounded and weary, and you are also fatigued. We all need rest now. Let us recover tonight and face them together in the morning."

Just then, some hunters, exhausted and in search of water, arrived at the lake. They were the same hunters who regularly brought meat to Bhima. Hiding nearby, they overheard the conversation between Duryodhana and Ashwatthama. Realizing that Duryodhana was hiding in the lake, they went straight to Bhima and told him everything. Bhima rewarded them generously and informed Yudhishthira. The Pandavas then proceeded to Dwaipayana Lake. Upon seeing them, Ashwatthama quietly withdrew.

***

Surya, Krishna, and Arijit were sitting in the lounge at Kolkata Airport. It was time for the security check.

"I want to have some coffee," Krishna said.

"I won't. Don't bring any for me," Surya replied.

"I don't want any either," added Arijit.

Krishna went to get the coffee. While he was returning, someone walking past him discreetly slipped a piece of paper into his trouser pocket. The message on the paper read: *"It's a futile effort. You can't save him. But you can go—Hyderabad is a beautiful place."*

Krishna showed the note to Surya and Arijit.

"Couldn't you catch the person who put it in your pocket?" Arijit asked.

"No, it all happened so quickly," Krishna said.

"It doesn't matter. They're very cautious," Surya remarked.

"It's time for a direct confrontation now," said Arijit.

The boarding announcement was made, and they got in line. Krishna and Surya sat next to each other, with Arijit seated right behind them.

"The person who put that note in your pocket is probably on this flight—and he might not be alone," Surya said quietly.

"How would you even recognize them?" Krishna asked.

"We'll discuss it later. For now, have some juice," Surya replied.

***

"Hey, Bijit da, it's been a while since we last spoke," Siddharth said after answering the call.

"Listen, I'm coming to your place today," Bijit replied.

"That's great! You're always welcome," Siddharth said cheerfully.

After hanging up, Siddharth began to wonder, "Why is Bijit da suddenly coming over. His voice sounded a bit unusual."

Siddharth was a distant relative of Bijit. He was a bachelor living alone in Hyderabad with a good job and a handsome salary. He used to visit Bijit's house often. But over time, as work took over, their contact had gradually diminished.

When Bijit arrived, Siddharth welcomed him in, offered him a seat, and said, "You have come here after a long time?"

"I've come alone this time, just for a short trip," Bijit replied.

"Alone? Is everything alright?"

"Yes, yes, everything's fine. I'm actually here for a job and thought of paying a visit to your house," Bijit explained.

"That's wonderful. Come, have something to eat. I cook pretty well these days..."

"But I'll only stay for a little while," Bijit said again.

"Come on, stay a few days! It'll be fun," Siddharth urged with a smile.

***

Surya and company checked into a good hotel. Arijit had arranged everything for them. Before entering the hotel room, Surya had roamed around for a while.

"What is your *dada* doing? He doesn't say anything," Arijit said to Krishna.

"He won't reveal anything now," Krishna replied.

***

Siddharth had left for the office, leaving Bijit alone. There was some tea in the flask. He was watching TV while enjoying a cup of tea with a bowl of *chanachur*. But how long could he keep hiding like this? He had to think of something. If proper security arrangements could be made… but for how many days would they be effective? He could only hope the killers would not find him there.

But who were they? Why did they want to kill him—or had already killed others? Was it revenge for that old incident? Several thoughts were going through his mind.

Suddenly, his mobile rang, snapping him back to reality.

"Hello—"

"Where do you think you can run? Heaven, earth, or the underworld—wherever you go, I will find you."

"Who… who are you? How did you get this number?"

"I'm the one whose entire family you destroyed. And no matter how many times you change your number, I'll track it down. Now it's your turn to leave this world."

"No, no…"

"So afraid of dying? Coward! I didn't see that fear back then! Well, get ready to face the ultimate consequence."

The call ended.

Bijit sat frozen, stunned.

They had found him out, and now, he had no choice but to leave this place immediately.

***

In the afternoon, Siddharth returned and asked, "Bijit da, are you feeling unwell?"

"No, no..." Bijit replied.

"By the way, I have lost my mobile phone again," Siddharth added.

Now Bijit realized how they had managed to get his number.

***

Upon reaching the shore of Dwaipayana Lake, Yudhishthira said to Krishna, "Look, Duryodhana has used *maya* to still the water and hide within it. But I will not let this deceiver escape."

Krishna replied, "A deceiver has to be defeated with *maya*. You, too, must kill Duryodhana in a cunning way."

Then Yudhishthira called out to Duryodhana, "Arise and face us in battle. Where is your pride now? Why do you flee and hide while your relatives and friends have laid down their lives on the battlefield? Why such fear of death? Cast it aside and fight!"

From within the lake, Duryodhana replied, "I have not fled out of fear. I have no chariot, no charioteer, no weapon—not even a blade of grass. I am alone and helpless. I have taken refuge in this lake merely to rest. When I am ready, I will rise and face you all in battle."

Yudhishthira responded, "Very well. Then rise now and fight."

Duryodhana replied again, "My brothers, my kinsmen, all the valiant warriors are dead. Our vast wealth has also been destroyed. I no longer have any desire for battle. I do not want the kingdom. I will go to the forest and live in peace. You may rule the kingdom."

Yudhishthira said sternly, "Even if you offer us the entire world, we will not accept it as a gift. I wish to claim the kingdom by defeating you in battle. And who are you to give anything—when you no longer even possess a kingdom? When we asked peacefully, you denied us even the amount of land that could fit on the tip of a needle. And now you offer the whole world? Your life is in our hands now. Now, get up and fight."

***

After breakfast, Surya said, "I'm going for a walk."

"We'll go with you," Krishna replied.

"No, if everyone comes along, it might create a problem," Surya said as he walked away.

"Come on, let's go too," Arijit said.

***

"I can't stay here any longer. I have to leave," said Bijit.

"Why? Is something wrong?" Siddharth asked anxiously.

"Oh no, nothing like that. It's just a very urgent and confidential matter. I'll explain everything later. And don't try calling this number—I won't be reachable. I'll contact you when I can," Bijit replied.

"Alright, what else can we do? It was nice having you here," Siddharth said with a sigh of resignation.

"One more thing—if anyone asks about me, don't mention that I was here. Okay?" Bijit added.

He booked a cab and left. But what he did not realize was that another car had started following him.

After a long drive, Bijit got off in a remote area far from the main city. He checked into a modest hotel and decided to lie low for a while.

The man tailing him observed everything. With a faint, sinister smile, he muttered to himself, "It's not so easy to escape us. You will have to die."

Meanwhile, Bijit believed he had finally found a place where no one could track him down.

***

Siddharth was sitting and thinking about Bijit. He felt a sense of comfort now that Bijit had come—the monotony of his lonely life was beginning to break. But who knew what urgent matter had pulled him away so suddenly?

At the sound of the doorbell, Siddharth opened the door and saw a man standing there.

"Is Bijit Babu here?" the man asked.

"No, he has already left. And you are?"

"I'm Surya Chatterjee, a private investigator. May I come in and speak with you?"

"Yes, of course. Please come in."

Surya entered and sat down on the sofa. "Can you tell me where he went?" he asked.

"He didn't say anything. But what's going on?"

"His life is in danger," Surya said grimly. "There's an assassin out to kill him, and he's on the run, trying to save himself. We're here to help him, but he isn't cooperating. He's trying to hide on his own. Meanwhile, his brother and a few others have already been killed—with arrows."

"That's horrifying!" Siddharth exclaimed.

"Yes, it truly is. So you honestly have no idea where he's gone?"

"No, I really don't. You have to trust me," Siddharth replied.

"Alright. If you learn anything, please let me know. Here's my mobile number."

Siddharth saved Surya's number and gave him his own in return.

"Take care," Surya said as he got up to leave.

***

From Siddharth's house, Surya went to a restaurant and ordered tea and some snacks. Just then, his mobile phone rang. Answering the call in Hindi, he asked, "What's the news there?"

The person on the other end said something.

"Alright, thank you," Surya replied, then turned his attention back to his food.

***

When Surya returned to the hotel, Krishna and Arijit looked at him with questioning eyes.

"I've never had Hyderabadi biryani before. I really want to try it. Let's have it today," he said.

"What happened?" Krishna asked.

"We're checking out tomorrow morning. You'll know everything then. For now, let's have Hyderabadi biryani."

After dinner, Surya said, "That was delicious. Make it some time and treat us."

"Of course I will. But don't keep us in the dark any longer," Krishna replied.

"I told you—you'll know everything tomorrow morning," Surya said.

***

The next morning, they left early, taking a car from the hotel along with a packed breakfast.

"We'll go to Hotel Krishna," Surya told the driver.

"Okay, sir," the driver replied.

The car stopped in front of Hotel Krishna. Surya made a phone call and spoke briefly. Then he turned to the others and said, "They'll be here shortly. Let's sit and have breakfast while we wait."

"Who's coming?" Krishna asked.

"You'll find out soon," Surya replied with a mysterious smile.

They quickly finished their breakfast. About half an hour later, a black car arrived, and two men stepped out. The car remained parked. As soon as it started moving again, Surya instructed their driver to follow.

"This is getting quite exciting," Krishna remarked.

"Arijit Babu, why are you so quiet?" Surya asked.

"Just like that. I'm watching everything," Arijit replied.

"Are you upset?" Surya inquired.

"No, not at all. Why would I be upset?" Arijit said.

The black car halted in front of another hotel. Surya's car stopped a little further away.

"Bijit is staying in this hotel now," Surya informed them.

Before anyone could react, the black car sped away.

"It looked like the attackers were in that car, right?" Krishna said.

"You're absolutely right."

"But they escaped. Shouldn't we go after them?" Arijit asked.

"There's no point. They realized we were tailing them and fled. By now, they're long gone. But they'll return—they can't accept that their mission has failed," Surya explained.

"So their goal was to kill Bijit?" Arijit asked.

"Yes. Our arrival foiled their plan."

They went to the hotel reception and showed Bijit's photo. The staff provided the room number. Arijit introduced himself as police.

They rang the doorbell, and after a moment, Bijit opened the door.

"Who are you?" he asked.

"We've finally found you," Surya said.

"Please, come in and sit down. Should I order some coffee?"

"Of course. And some snacks, too," Krishna added.

"Okay," Bijit agreed and placed the order.

"It's not just us—your enemies have also found out about your new location," Surya warned.

"Is that so?" Bijit asked, fear flashing in his eyes.

"Yes. You can see how sophisticated their operation is," Surya said.

"They clearly have a strong network," Krishna observed.

"Exactly. Now, tell me—do you want to keep running, or will you come back to Kolkata with us under our protection? Time is short. The enemy could strike again at any moment. I've recognized them, and I'll try to catch them," Surya assured him.

Arijit looked at him thoughtfully.

"I have an idea," Bijit said.

"What is it?" Arijit asked.

"I'm planning to go abroad. A friend of mine is organizing a European tour. I said I'd join. He's working on arranging my visa quickly."

"Not a bad idea. Can we join you? We'd love to explore Europe as well. Maybe your friend can help with our arrangements, too?"

"Sure, but you'll need valid passports."

"First, we'll return to Kolkata with you. Then we'll make further plans. You can't stay here any longer—it's not safe. Come stay with us at our hotel for now."

"But I can't join you in the European tour," Arijit said.

"Alright then, focus on tracking down the attackers. I have their pictures—I'll give them to you."

"You've done a lot of groundwork already," Arijit said, impressed.

"Surya Babu is a genius," Bijit added. "He always delivers on his promises."

They quickly got into the car with Bijit. Just then, there was a loud sound, and an arrow struck the car window.

"Look!" Arijit was about to jump out.

Surya stopped him. "Don't. It's too dangerous. They're professionals. It's safer to stay in the car."

The car sped away.

***

"You saw how dangerous they were," Surya said to Bijit.

"That's why I had instructed the hotel staff not to allow anyone into my room. They let you in only because you introduced yourselves as policemen."

"They could have entered the room by some other means," Arijit added.

"Alright, I'm asking again—look at their pictures. Did you have any enmity with them?" Surya asked.

Bijit remained silent.

"If you don't share everything with us, we won't be able to protect you," Surya warned.

Back in Kolkata, Bijit was accommodated in his own house, with two policemen assigned to guard him.

"You must not go anywhere without informing us, no matter how important the matter may be," Arijit instructed.

"Alright, I admit it—going to Hyderabad was a mistake. It didn't help at all," Bijit conceded.

"Let bygones be bygones. There's no point crying over spilt milk," Krishna said.

In the meantime, nothing new occurred. Everyone received their visas, and it was time to travel to Europe.

"We haven't seen any further activity from the attackers," Krishna observed.

"Yes," Surya agreed. "Arijit will continue trying to catch them. Let's see what happens."

***

Krishna, Surya, and Bijit joined the rest of the group at the airport. There were twenty-five people in total.

"That's good. It's not easy to do anything when surrounded by so many people," Surya said.

"Do you think they'll follow us here too?" Krishna asked.

"They might. Nothing is impossible."

Since arriving, Bijit had become noticeably more relaxed.

Their destination was London, with a stopover in Bahrain. The journey was exhausting. While browsing the shops at the Bahrain airport, someone suddenly placed a hand on Krishna's shoulder. Startled, Krishna turned around and saw a tall man who said coldly, "We've come here too. We'll kill him. Save him if you can."

With that, the man walked away briskly. Despite the hat partially obscuring his face, it was obvious he was one of the two men Surya had shown them earlier.

Krishna immediately informed Surya.

"I told you—they won't let him go that easily," Surya said grimly.

"He's openly threatening us! How dare he! But how did he even get a visa?" asked Krishna.

"Somehow… Anyway, let's go. It's time to catch our connecting flight," said Surya.

"Yes, let's go," said Krishna.

Once on the plane, Krishna began scanning the cabin for any sign of the attackers.

"Krishna, you don't need to keep looking around so anxiously," Surya said calmly.

***

When they arrived at Heathrow Airport, their local guide, Anjali, greeted them warmly.

"Welcome to London," she said with a smile.

After completing all the formalities, the group gathered outside the airport. A cool breeze was blowing, and a light rain had begun to fall. Many passers-by were holding long umbrellas.

"It feels great, doesn't it?" Krishna said.

"Yes, very nice," someone replied.

Soon, their bus arrived, and everyone boarded. Just then, the rain stopped, and the sun emerged.

"This is typical English weather—sunny one moment, rainy the next," said Surya.

"That's why everyone's carrying an umbrella," Krishna added with a smile.

As the bus rolled on, the group members began to interact and get to know each other. There were two more Bengalis sitting near them, while the rest of the group included people from South India, Delhi, Uttar Pradesh, and Rajasthan.

A gentleman named Vishal Agrawal struck up a conversation with Krishna. He was a businessman familiar with Kolkata.

"The *mishti doi* and *rasgulla* from Kolkata are legendary," he told Krishna.

After checking into the hotel, everyone retired to their rooms. Surya and Krishna shared one room, while Bijit was placed with a Tamil gentleman named Mr. Krishnamurthy in the room next door.

"It's good that Bijit Babu is sharing a room," Surya commented. Then, turning to Bijit, he added, "Make sure you inspect the room carefully before locking or unlocking the door."

"Of course," Bijit replied reassuringly.

Everyone was exhausted. In each room, there was a coffee maker. After preparing some coffee, Surya and Krishna lay down to rest.

Later, when Krishna woke up, he said, "Come on, let's go for a walk."

"No, absolutely not. The enemy might be nearby. We have to be very careful," Surya warned.

"Sorry, I completely forgot," Krishna said apologetically.

After a light dinner that evening, everyone went to bed. The next morning, they woke up and got ready for the day.

"We should have breakfast now," Krishna said. "We can meet the rest of the group there."

"I see they're serving Darjeeling tea as well," Surya noted.

"It's a wonderful arrangement," said a man in fluent Bengali. "I'm Ramesh Upadhyay. I'm originally from Kolkata but now live in Delhi."

Surya and Krishna introduced themselves in return.

Soon after, Anjali addressed the group: "In a short while, we will check out and begin our city tour. Everyone, please get ready."

"Look over there," Surya said.

Krishna turned and saw Bijit sitting quietly, focused on his breakfast. Surya walked up to him and said, "Good morning."

"Good morning. Have you had your breakfast?" Bijit asked.

"Yes, we have. Did you sleep well last night?" Surya asked.

"Yes, I did. I feel much safer here. I really hope those two won't be able to reach me, and on the way back there, Arijit Babu will definitely catch them."

"They're here too," Surya said gravely.

"What? That's terrible!" Bijit exclaimed, visibly shaken.

Surya and Krishna walked away to load their luggage into the coach.

"You've really scared him," Krishna remarked.

"He should be scared. He must have done something awful in the past—bad enough for people to follow him all the way to Europe to kill him," said Surya.

"But he's not saying anything," said Krishna.

Once everyone's luggage was loaded into the storage compartment, they took their seats on the bus.

"Good morning, everyone," Anjali called out cheerfully. "Our city tour begins now. Did you all sleep well?"

"Yes," the group responded in unison.

"Great!" Anjali said with a smile.

Their sightseeing tour began with some of London's iconic locations. They stopped at Buckingham Palace, the residence and administrative headquarters of the British royal family, located in Westminster. Built in 1703 for the Duke of Buckingham, the palace features a famous balcony at its eastern end, where the royal family appears during major events. Some of the rooms are open to the public on special occasions.

The tourists admired the palace from outside and took several photos.

"Come on, let's take a selfie," Krishna called to Surya.

Nearby, some performers dressed as Roman gladiators were posing with tourists—for a fee.

Bijit stood at a distance, looking around nervously.

"He's absolutely terrified," Krishna said.

After visiting several landmarks, everyone returned to the bus. Along the way, they saw the River Thames, London Bridge, Big Ben, the London Eye, Trafalgar Square, and many stunning sculptures.

The Thames is the longest river in England, flowing through the southern part of the country. It's also known as the Isis River. Big Ben, a towering clock, is renowned for its grandeur and elegance. Trafalgar Square, located in Westminster, was built to commemorate Britain's victory over France and Spain at the Battle of Trafalgar. It serves as a gathering place for the public, where various events, including Christmas celebrations, are held.

"When you're in a place like this, observe everything with full attention," Surya advised Krishna.

The London Eye, formerly called the Millennium Wheel, is a giant rotating observation wheel offering panoramic views of London.

Around noon, they grabbed a quick bite. The tour package included breakfast and dinner, but lunch had to be arranged by the travellers themselves.

Later, the bus entered a train that travelled through an underwater tunnel, taking the tourists to France.

"What an experience!" Krishna exclaimed in amazement.

Upon reaching Paris, they checked into their hotel, had dinner, and went to sleep.

The next morning, after breakfast, they set out to explore the city.

"You see, they don't understand English," Krishna remarked. "Even basic words like salt, sugar, or eggs need to be said in French."

"Or maybe they just don't want to understand," Surya replied.

"Maybe. But Bijit Babu looks quite gloomy," Krishna noted.

"It's understandable, given his mental state. The threat could come at any moment," Surya said.

"But we haven't seen them yet," Krishna pointed out.

"Why? Do you *want* to see them? It's better if you don't," Surya warned.

"But—" Before Krishna could complete his sentence, Surya motioned him to stay silent.

***

Paris is a city known for its art and fashion. The streets are lined with shops and roadside cafés, where people enjoy eating and drinking while sitting on chairs outside. It is quite crowded, and the atmosphere is lively.

"Very nice," said Pande Ji, who was from Allahabad.

They visited the Grevin Wax Museum, which houses wax statues of many famous personalities—sportsmen, statesmen, film stars, singers, painters, sculptors, and others.

"There's even a statue of Mahatma Gandhi here!" Krishna exclaimed.

There was no restriction on taking pictures inside the museum. Surya kept a close watch on Bijit, but nothing unusual happened. Afterwards, they left the wax museum.

***

"It's very nice," said Surya.

Next, they visited the world-famous Louvre Museum, one of the top tourist attractions in Paris and the largest art museum in the world. Originally constructed as a fortress, the Louvre was later rebuilt into a royal palace and eventually opened to the public as a museum. During Napoleon Bonaparte's reign, the museum was temporarily renamed. Later, during World War II, Nazi forces occupied Paris and took over the museum. However, before their arrival, most of the museum's valuable items had already been relocated to a safe place. When the Nazis arrived, they found the museum empty and used it as a clearing house.

The museum houses an extraordinary collection of paintings, sculptures, and other artworks. Tourists are overwhelmed by the grandeur and richness of the exhibits.

"Come on, I'll show you the world-famous *Mona Lisa*," said Mary, the French guide.

Standing in front of the painting, she explained, "The *Mona Lisa* was painted by the renowned Italian philosopher, sculptor, and artist Leonardo da Vinci. The work was likely completed in 1506. It is the most famous and widely discussed painting in the world. What makes it so special is the mysterious smile of Mona Lisa. The woman portrayed in the painting is believed to be La Gioconda, the wife of Francesco del Giocondo. According to historical records, the painting was commissioned to celebrate their move to a new home and the birth of their second child.

"The smile is considered an optical illusion. When your gaze shifts from her eyes to her lips, it appears as though she's smiling. Interestingly, this painting was once stolen."

"Really?" Pande ji exclaimed.

"Yes," Mary replied with a smile. Though French, she spoke fluent English. "It was stolen in 1911 by an Italian thief."

Everyone stood staring at the painting in stunned silence.

Suddenly, Krishna noticed that Surya was missing. Looking around, he spotted someone speaking with him a little distance away.

"Hey, that's one of the murderers," Krishna said in surprise.

The man handed Surya a small diary, gave Krishna a faint smile, waved, and walked away.

As Krishna was about to speak, Surya interrupted, "Don't ask anything right now. Be patient—you'll get all the answers. For now, observe everything carefully. You're an artist; your eyes see differently."

Krishna understood that he would not get any answers at the moment.

Surya continued, "You need to stay close to Bijit Babu and take care of him."

"There's no need. Nothing will happen to him here. Don't wander off like that, okay?" Krishna replied.

After leaving the Louvre, they went to McDonald's and had burgers and coffee.

"My stomach doesn't feel full unless I have rice and dal at noon," said Ushanath Babu, who was from Asansol.

"That's exactly what you said earlier, Uncle. And don't forget potato poppy and fish curry," Krishna added.

Surya smiled to himself, thinking, *Krishna seems to have quite a few uncles.*

"And why leave out chutneys, papads, curd, and sweets?" added Jayashree from Howrah with a cheerful smile.

"Oh yes, I'll eat everything when I visit your home," said Krishna.

"Alright, I'll make sure you're fed to your heart's content," replied Jayashree with a grin.

***

Bijit was feeling a little better now.

"We're now going to see the Eiffel Tower—one of the wonders of the world," the guide announced.

The Eiffel Tower is considered the symbol of both France and Paris. Built in 1889, it was named after Gustave Eiffel, whose company designed the structure. Made of wrought iron, it was constructed to commemorate the centenary of the French Revolution and was inaugurated by the Prince of Wales from Britain. Standing at 1,063 feet, it is roughly as tall as an 81-story building.

The Eiffel Tower has three levels: the first floor, the second floor, and the summit at the top. After buying their tickets, the tourists entered the tower. Krishna climbed up and exclaimed, "Amazing! What a fantastic view!"

"Take a good photo," Surya reminded him.

Nearby, there was a board where visitors were writing comments. Bijit stood in front of it. Just then, someone whispered to him, "Write something on the board—because after this, you have to leave this world."

Startled, Bijit looked up and saw one of the two men who had earlier tried to kill him.

"Goodbye," the man said and disappeared.

Bijit's face turned pale, and he looked visibly shaken.

Seeing his condition, Surya asked, "What happened? Why do you look like that?"

"The enemy showed up and told me my death is near," Bijit replied.

"Alright, come with us," said Surya.

They descended and returned to the hotel. On the way back, Pande ji and Jayashree lifted everyone's spirits by singing on the bus.

After having dinner, when they entered their hotel room, Krishna said, "Bijit Babu's condition has worsened."

"What more can we do for him?" Surya asked.

"It seems they're toying with him before they kill him," Krishna said grimly.

"Exactly. Anyway, let's go to bed now—I need a good night's sleep," said Surya.

***

The next day, they were headed to Switzerland—another dream destination.

"The breakfast in London was really good. What more can I say?" Jayashree said to Krishna.

"That was probably the highlight. The longer the trip goes on, the worse things might get," Krishna replied.

Everyone gathered with their luggage, and soon, the bus began moving. The journey was long, but the scenic beauty on both sides made it enjoyable. Besides Pande Ji and Jayashree, one or two others also sang during the ride. As they neared Switzerland, the temperature gradually dropped. At last, they arrived at their much-anticipated destination.

The hotel was stunning. A short distance away, there was a small library filled with books from around the world, and next to it stood a piano open for anyone to play.

Surya's room was quite nice as well; the snow-covered peaks of the Alps were visible through the window.

"Let's take a look outside," Surya suggested.

"Yes, let's go," Krishna agreed.

It was dark and bitterly cold outside. They quickly put on their jackets and stepped out, taking Bijit along, though he was reluctant to come.

"It's really cold," Bijit muttered.

"After death, the body becomes cold," someone said nearby and walked away.

"That's him!" Bijit exclaimed, his eyes wide with panic. "I want to go home," he added and hurried back to the hotel.

"Let's go too. It's starting to rain," Surya said.

Dinner was quite satisfying. Later, Surya sat in his room reading the diary given to him by one of the murderers while Krishna flipped through the pictures he had taken during the day.

***

The next morning, they set off for Jungfrau. Everyone stepped off the bus and headed toward the elevator. Delicate snowflakes were floating in the air. Bundled in thick sweaters, jackets, and gloves, the group braced themselves against the biting cold of the alpine weather.

The elevator ride began, slowly ascending through a landscape blanketed in snow and ice. Below, a layer of silvery frost clung to fallen pine needles, creating a picture-perfect winter scene.

"This is a wonderful experience," Mr. Krishnamurthy said, his eyes gleaming.

"Absolutely," Mr. Malhotra agreed, nodding in admiration.

Soon, they reached the top — a magical realm that could only be described as an ice kingdom. A snowman sculpted from solid ice stood cheerfully in one corner. It was time for the next adventure: a ride on the cable car.

Bijit was reluctant to go.

Krishna and Surya went ahead, stepping into the cable car as it began to glide over the vast expanse of snow.

"Bijit Babu is afraid of cable cars," Krishna said with a teasing smile.

"It's perfectly natural to be scared," Surya replied gently.

After they got off the cable car, they wandered for a while, crunching over the icy surface. Soon, they reached the Sphinx Observatory. From there, breath-taking views stretched out in every direction — snow-capped peaks, sprawling glaciers, and the pristine wilderness.

"This is incredibly beautiful," Surya said in awe as Krishna got busy snapping pictures.

Next, they explored the famous Ice Palace, a marvel built by a mountain guide. Inside were vaulted rooms and tunnels filled with enchanting ice sculptures — penguins, birds, bears, people, cars, and furniture — all carved from crystal-clear ice. It was like stepping into a frozen fairy tale.

Later, they continued their journey to Lucerne. Krishna and Surya took the chance to buy authentic Swiss watches, while Bijit remained disinterested, showing little enthusiasm for anything.

On the way back, their guide shared interesting facts about Switzerland. Most Swiss people are of German origin, but the population also includes Italians, French, and a small group of Romans. The German spoken here has a regional flavour known as Swiss German. Most of the original inhabitants trace their roots back to the Great Migration of Nations around 400 AD, which followed the fall of the Roman Empire. In addition to German, French, Italian, and Romansh are also spoken in Switzerland. The national currency is the Swiss franc. The country is also renowned for its chocolate, watches, cuckoo clocks, and the majestic views of the Alps. It's also home to the world-famous Swiss banks.

After dinner, they returned to the hotel. Surya headed to his room and called Ujjaini.

"How are things going? I hope everything's fine. Don't forget to send me the pictures," Ujjaini said.

"I will," replied Surya.

"Are you okay?" she asked.

"We've made good progress. Just waiting for the end now," he answered.

"And Krishna?" she asked with a laugh.

"He's been busy wandering around and taking photos," Surya said with a smile.

"Great! Tell me all the stories when you're back," she said warmly.

Surya then spoke to his sister, Srija.

"Is everything alright? You all need to be very careful," she warned.

"We're okay. How about you? Where's Tiyasha?" Surya asked.

"She's here, hold on. I'll put her on the phone," said Srija.

"Uncle, take care of yourself, and may your mission be successful," said Tiyasha sweetly.

"*Baba*, you've grown up so much!" Surya chuckled affectionately.

Surya also got in touch with Arijit.

"What's the update, boss?" Arijit asked, sounding eager.

"Bijit Babu is safe. No problems on that front. Were you able to catch the murderers?" Surya inquired.

"Not yet. I'm working on it," Arijit replied.

"Try to get them before we're back," Surya said firmly.

After ending the call, Krishna turned to Surya. "Don't you want to tell Arijit that they've arrived here too?"

"You're right," Surya said thoughtfully.

"But why aren't we catching them even though we know that they are here," Krishna asked in frustration.

"It's not that simple," Surya explained. "We're in a foreign country. The local police may not cooperate. And..." he paused.

"And what?" Krishna pressed.

"Bijit Babu isn't exactly innocent. He's facing the consequences of his past. I believe the attackers are waiting for the right moment — they'll probably strike toward the end of this trip. For now, they're just playing psychological games. I'll let you read the diary they gave me yesterday. It will explain a lot," Surya said.

Their next destination was Italy. After a long journey, they finally arrived in Rome — the historic and vibrant capital of the country.

They decided to rest for the night and explore the city the following morning.

"When will you give me the diary to read?" Krishna asked eagerly.

"After dinner," Surya promised.

True to his word, after dinner, Surya returned to their hotel room and handed Krishna the diary. Krishna took it with great anticipation and began reading intently.

***

This is my story, a story of betrayal and conspiracy. It reveals how greed can strip people of their humanity and drive them to unimaginable cruelty.

My name is Shubhabrata Chowdhury. My elder brother, Tapobrata Chowdhury, was a renowned doctor. His wife, Amrita, was a kind-hearted woman, and their son, little

Roni, was full of life. I was deeply attached to Roni. *Dada* was always busy with work and could not spend much time with him, so I became Roni's closest companion. We shared laughter, stories, and moments I still cherish.

I had just started a new job after completing my engineering degree. Our father, Birendra Chowdhury, a respected lawyer, had amassed considerable wealth and had chosen to transfer it all to *dada*. We lived comfortably and happily under one roof.

My father's elder brother, Nrisingha Chowdhury, was not as fortunate. He held no significant position. His sons, Bijit and Sujit, had grown up facing hardship, and it bred a deep-seated jealousy in them—one they barely concealed. But *dada* was too naive to understand it. Both he and *boudi* were good-natured to a fault, and people often took advantage of their kindness.

One person who always looked out for us was our manager, Arpan da. He managed our affairs with diligence and affection and cared for me like an elder brother. He still stands by me today.

Then, there was our uncle, Shameek Dutta Roy, who lived in Beleghata. He had squandered his ancestral property due to greed and poor choices and even borrowed money from *dada*. One day, he invited us to his home. I did not want to go, but *dada* insisted, so I joined him, *boudi*, and Roni.

We were welcomed warmly, though I immediately sensed something was wrong. Aside from Bijit and Sujit, others had gathered—Anirban da, Bijit's uncle Animesh Dasgupta (a lawyer), and their relative, Ranajoy Sarkar. It felt strange. Shameek was known for being stingy. Why would he host such a crowd?

We were seated when suddenly Animesh approached *dada* with a document.

"Just sign here quickly," he said.

Dada, taken aback, asked, "What's this about? Why should I sign anything?"

"Oh, nothing important. You're just transferring power of attorney for your property to Bijit," he said casually.

Dada was stunned. "Why would I do that?"

"If you don't, your son will die," Ranajoy growled, pressing a gleaming knife to Roni's throat.

"No! Please don't hurt him—I'll sign!" *dada* cried.

"That's like a good boy," came the mocking reply.

"*Dada,* don't sign!" I shouted, trying to rush forward, but four men restrained me. They were outsiders, clearly part of the plot.

The moment *dada* signed, Ranajoy stabbed Roni to death. And with the same knife, Sujit da murdered *dada* and *boudi*. I was helpless, screaming inside, frozen with unbearable pain.

They wiped the knife clean, wrapped it in a handkerchief, and forced it into my hand—then dropped it on the floor.

"Everything is going as planned," Animesh said coolly.

Uncle Shameek called the police, and when they arrived, he told them I had killed everyone in a fit of rage after a heated argument with *dada*. He claimed I picked a cleaver from the kitchen and went on a rampage. The police found the knife, smeared with my fingerprints, and arrested me.

I was shattered, grief-stricken and powerless. Animesh built a strong case against me. Later, Arpan da learned the full extent of the conspiracy. They had lured Shameek into the plot with promises of wealth. *Jethu* Nrisingha Chowdhury knew everything yet stood by silently. His silence made him just as guilty.

They took over our property without question. No one wondered why *dada* would suddenly hand over everything to Bijit. They even bribed the lawyer Arpan da had hired to defend me. All the false testimonies and fabricated evidence sealed my fate.

Arpan da told me that the entire scheme was orchestrated by Anirban and Animesh.

And then came their next lie—that *dada* had willingly signed over the property to Bijit before leaving on a tour, and I, unhappy with that decision, killed everyone in anger.

The court believed them. I was sentenced to life in prison. I still remember the smug satisfaction on their faces when the verdict was announced. Only Arpan da stood by me. A man of true character, he visited often and gave me hope.

"We will get justice," he promised.

I held on to that vow. Over time, due to my good conduct in prison—teaching, organizing cultural programmes, and even giving computer lessons—I was released early.

After my release, I stayed with Arpan da. He had kept track of everyone involved. The entire episode reminded me of the Mahabharata. So, I became Dhananjaya, and he was my Vasudeva.

Bijit and Sujit were Duryodhana and Dushasana. Anirban was Karna, Nrisingha was Dhritarashtra, Animesh was Shakuni, Ranajoy was Jayadratha, and Shameek was Shalya.

I took up archery. I trained in silence. And then, one by one, I made them pay.

Ranajoy came first—the man who killed my beloved nephew. I disguised myself as his manager, threatened him, and then ended his life. He deserved no mercy.

Next was Sujit—the traitor who murdered his own brother and sister-in-law. I killed him on a public road. It was risky, but I pulled it off.

Then came Anirban. I struck him down in the garden of his own house. A fitting end for a man so vile.

After that, it was Shameek's turn. He betrayed blood for greed. I scared him first, and then killed him.

Animesh, the mastermind, was next. I played tricks to terrify him—recorded voices and eerie messages from his son's phone. He fled to Puri, but I found him. I ended his life with an arrow.

Now, only Bijit remains. But there's a complication. The famous detective Surya Chatterjee and his assistant Krishna are on the case—and they've figured us out.

Well done to them. But they still can't stop what's coming.

Bijit will die one way or another. We won't touch Nrisingha—let him live with the grief of losing his son. That will be his punishment. I told him so myself when I visited him in the hospital.

I no longer call them *jethu, dada,* or *mama*. Those titles are sacred—and they have defiled them.

If you're reading this diary, I hope you understand why I did what I did. Step aside if you must. But even if you don't, it won't matter.

We will finish what we started. This is no longer just revenge.

This is a righteous war.

***

The diary had come to an end. The handwriting was large and elegant, almost beautiful to look at. After reading it, Krishna said thoughtfully, "After going through this, I truly feel they're doing the right thing. People like that deserve such a fate. They have my full support."

"I knew you'd say that," Surya replied with a slight smile. "But as someone who stands by the law, I can't openly agree. Still… I do feel a certain sympathy for them. And honestly, you're not wrong in what you said earlier."

Krishna leaned in. "I get it. But tell me—how did you figure out they were behind all this?"

"Easy, my friend. One step at a time," Surya said, cutting him off gently. "There's a time for everything, and this isn't it. Let's call it a night—it's already quite late."

***

The next morning, they set off for Rome. Unfortunately, the breakfast was far from satisfying, and Krishna's pale face showed his disappointment.

Rome—an ancient city steeped in history—is the capital of Italy. Every corner seems to whisper stories of the past. Once the heart of the mighty Roman Empire, its legacy still looms large. According to legend, the city was named after Romulus, the Roman emperor who was believed to have founded it.

That timeless aura was everywhere. Their first destination was Vatican City.

Vatican City is a sovereign nation—the only country in the world located entirely within another city. It is the spiritual and administrative headquarters of the Roman Catholic Church and is ruled by the Pope. The city also houses a magnificent museum filled with exquisite Roman sculptures.

They entered through a long, winding queue. Bijit, however, remained on the bus with one or two others.

"His condition is really bad," said Surya.

"As the action, so the result," Krishna replied quietly.

While the rest of the group explored, Surya and Krishna wandered around, sipping fruit juice and munching burgers from Indian food stalls. A few Bangladeshi street vendors were selling souvenirs nearby. Tourists from all over the world filled the streets.

In many spots, performers dressed as ancient knights posed with visitors for money. Nearby stood broken pillars and scattered ruins—remnants of a once-glorious civilization.

Next, they made their way to the Colosseum. The entrance queue here was equally massive, but this time, Bijit joined them.

The Colosseum, an oval-shaped amphitheatre in the heart of Rome, began construction in 69 AD and was completed in 81 AD. Built under the Roman emperors Vespasian and Titus—and later expanded by Domitian—it is also known as the Flavian Amphitheater, named after the ruling dynasty of that time. Today, it stands as a symbol of the Roman Empire, a wonder of the world, and one of Italy's most iconic landmarks.

It once held between 50,000 and 80,000 spectators, who came to witness brutal gladiator battles, wild animal hunts, public executions, and theatrical reenactments of legendary Roman events. The accused were often thrown before lions or other beasts, and the crowd watched the bloody spectacle with excitement. It was a cruel form of entertainment.

"Imagine two gladiators fighting to the death in this arena," Surya said, gazing at the vast structure.

"Yes—and one of them is Dhananjaya, the other Bijit," Krishna joked.

Surya burst out laughing.

In the early Middle Ages, these violent events came to an end. Over the centuries, the Colosseum was used for various other purposes. Earthquakes and the looting of its stones caused significant damage, but it still remains a major attraction.

"We've walked a lot today," Krishna said, stretching a bit.

"Yeah, let's grab some coffee," Surya suggested with a smile.

***

The next day, the tour group headed to Pisa—home of the world-famous Leaning Tower. Known for its distinct tilt, the tower leans noticeably to one side, which is exactly what makes it so iconic.

Their guide explained that the architect behind this structure was Bonanno Pisano. Legend has it that Galileo Galilei used the tower to conduct his experiments. Standing 56 meters tall, the tower has 294 steps spiralling to the top. Interestingly, the lean began after the second floor was constructed, all because of a shallow foundation built on soft, unstable soil. Though the design was flawed from the start, it has become a magnet for millions of curious visitors from around the world.

Krishna took a picture of the leaning tower above Surya's head.

"Let me try one like that. Stand right there," said Surya with a grin.

"*Aribba*! You're getting really good at this," Krishna laughed.

Meanwhile, Bijit was pacing nearby, looking a bit anxious.

Soon after, the group made their way to Florence.

***

Florence, the capital of Italy's Tuscany region, is a city steeped in history and renowned for its Renaissance art and architecture. Among its many treasures is Michelangelo's masterpiece *David*—a symbol of human perfection carved in marble. Surrounded by rolling hills dotted with elegant villas, lush vineyards, and olive orchards, Florence is as scenic as it is culturally rich. It is no surprise that the city has been declared a UNESCO World Heritage Site.

Florence has been home to many legendary figures, including Galileo, Leonardo da Vinci, Dante, Michelangelo, and Machiavelli. Even the famous explorer Amerigo Vespucci was also a native of this city. Often called the cradle of the Renaissance, the city still reflects the brilliance of that era in almost every corner.

The group visited Michelangelo's *David*, mesmerized by its beauty and precision.

"Look at the eyes and that intense posture," Surya observed.

"Yes, there's a bold defiance in his stance," Krishna agreed.

They posed for photos in front of the famed *Gates of Paradise*—the magnificent bronze doors of the Baptistery of San Giovanni, intricately decorated with scenes from the Old Testament.

Their sightseeing continued with visits to the Florence Cathedral, Signoria Square, Santa Maria Novella, and the iconic Brunelleschi's Dome.

"Let's try the famous Italian pizza," Surya suggested.

"Absolutely! We must," Krishna smiled, and then turned to Bijit. "What about you? Pizza?"

"No, I want to get some drink instead," Bijit replied and went to the other side.

As the day drew to a close, their guide announced, "Tomorrow, we head to Venice. Our tour of Florence is complete."

"Do you know the story of Shakespeare's *The Merchant of Venice*?" Surya asked Krishna.

"No, not really," Krishna admitted.

"Read it sometime. It's worth it," Surya replied.

Venice, the enchanting city built on more than a hundred small islands in the Adriatic Sea, awaited them. Separated by canals and connected by bridges, these islands are located in the magical Venetian Lagoon.

The next morning, they boarded a boat and set sail for Venice, ready for the next chapter of their Italian adventure.

***

As they made their way to Venice, Surya struck up a friendly conversation with an Italian gentleman. After some time, they arrived at their destination.

"Just like a painting!" Krishna exclaimed, wide-eyed with excitement.

"Here, the waterways are the roads," Surya explained. "Those boats you see floating are called gondolas, unique to Venice. Aren't they beautiful?"

They soon found themselves in the heart of the city at the spacious Piazza San Marco, home to the stunning St. Mark's Basilica and the Campanile bell tower.

Later, they visited the famous Murano Glass Factory, where delicate and colourful glass creations filled the displays.

"You know, photography is not allowed in here," Surya reminded gently.

"Alright, alright," Krishna replied sheepishly and stopped taking photos.

***

When the tour ended, they returned by boat. Their journey through Italy had come to a close, and their next destination was Austria.

After dinner, Bijit came to Surya's room.

"Please, have a seat," Surya said.

"I can't take it anymore," Bijit confessed, his voice trembling. "They've made my life miserable. I'm constantly afraid. I don't know when they'll strike next."

"Atonement for sins," Krishna murmured under his breath.

"What did you just say?" Bijit snapped, turning sharply before storming out of the room.

"You're speaking without understanding the gravity of the situation," Surya scolded Krishna.

"I just couldn't stay silent any longer," Krishna replied, looking down.

"Alright, let's leave it for now," Surya said, trying to defuse the tension.

The next morning at breakfast, Bijit kept his distance, avoiding them altogether.

***

Finally, the day of reckoning had come. Dhananjaya and Vasudeva approached Bijit, who was startled to see them. Without a word, they quietly led him to a secluded spot.

Surya noticed the unusual movement and gently signalled Krishna to follow them.

"What is it you want to say?" Bijit asked, his voice uneasy.

"Do you remember everything?" Dhananjaya replied.

Bijit's eyes widened. "You... you're Shubhabrata! And Arpan's with you! You two are behind all this!"

"Yes," Shubhabrata said calmly. "I've already taken care of the others. You're the last one left. Do you remember that day? You didn't even spare a child. No punishment could ever be enough for what you did. You have no shame—running away like a coward. Why don't you just die?"

With that, Shubhabrata or Dhananjaya and Arpan or Vasudeva turned and walked away, leaving Bijit frozen in place, shattered and stunned.

"Come on, Bijit Babu; it's time to go," Surya called out gently.

The journey from Italy to Austria was long. Inside the bus, soft music played. Pande ji was singing old Mohammed Rafi songs, and Mr. Krishnamurthy was also singing with a surprisingly melodious voice.

***

Duryodhana turned to Yudhishthira and said, "I am alone, wounded, without a chariot or weapons. You are many, armed and mounted. It will be fairer if you face me one at a time."

Yudhishthira replied calmly, "Then decide for yourself—choose anyone among us and any weapon you prefer. If you defeat him, the Kuru kingdom shall be yours."

Duryodhana declared, "I will fight with a mace. Whoever accepts my challenge must also fight with a mace." With those words, he rose from the water, sending ripples and echoes through the still air.

Bhima stepped forward, gripping his mace tightly. His eyes burned with fury as he said, "Remember your sins, Duryodhana. You have caused us a lot of suffering. Our grandfather Bhishma is lying on a bed of arrows, and so many great warriors have died—all because of you. Today, I will end it all. I will destroy you."

Duryodhana sneered, "Do not boast in vain. No one can defeat me in a mace duel. If it is war you want, I shall give it to you."

At that moment, Balarama arrived, having heard of the impending clash between Bhima and Duryodhana. He spoke solemnly, "Let this duel take place at Samanta Panchaka, within Kurukshetra. It is a sacred ground—worthy of such a battle."

Everyone then proceeded to the designated battlefield.

***

Nrisingha was lying restless on the bed, tossing and turning, his mind heavy with worry. There was still no news of his elder son—who knew what condition he was in or where he might be? A cold fear gripped him, fear of the unknown. The pain of losing his younger son still haunted him, and now memories of happier days came flooding back. Was he destined to carry the burden of sorrow alone? Was it now only his turn to weep?

***

Austria, nestled in the southern part of Central Europe, is a land of breathtaking beauty. Its capital, Vienna, stands as a cultural and historical gem. The country shares its borders with Germany, the Czech Republic, Slovakia, Hungary, Italy, and Switzerland. Much of Austria is mountainous, thanks to the majestic Alps.

The group's first destination was the famous Swarovski Crystal Worlds—a major attraction in Austria. Created by artist André Heller for Swarovski, the renowned crystal glass manufacturer, the site features a park, art museum, restaurant, and retail area. At the entrance stood the iconic "Giant," a striking sculpture that left visitors in awe.

"Come here, we have to take a selfie," Krishna said excitedly.

As they stepped inside, they were dazzled by the spectacle around them. Crystals glittered in every direction, in countless shapes and colours, creating a magical atmosphere. Everyone bought crystals, enchanted by their sparkling beauty. Surya, too, bought a few pieces.

After spending some time exploring, the group boarded the bus and continued their journey. Eventually, they stopped at a marketplace filled with small shops. Krishna and Surya bought cowboy hats from the market.

"Look, there are trams here too—just like ours," Surya said, smiling. "It feels good to see familiar things in a new land."

The bus resumed its journey but soon came to an unexpected halt. Something was wrong, and the driver began inspecting the vehicle. Everyone got off.

"Let's check what the problem is," said Mr. Krishnamurthy.

The surroundings were picturesque. The road sloped downward, revealing a stunning view of the mountains in the distance. As the others admired the landscape, Bijit quietly walked to the edge of the road.

"I'll go see what's going on," Surya said, following him.

"I have to die… I must die!" Bijit cried out suddenly—and before anyone could react, he jumped.

A wave of shock rippled through the group as people screamed in horror. The local guide quickly contacted the police. After a tense search, Bijit's lifeless body was found below, frozen and still.

Surya stood silently, grief-stricken. Krishna said nothing, his face pale and stunned.

The police carried out their formalities. It was clearly a suicide—everyone had witnessed it. Once the bus was repaired, the journey continued, but a heavy silence hung in the air.

"I wonder what sorrow haunted him so deeply that he chose to end his life in a foreign land," Jayashree murmured softly.

"There are so many hardships in life," Ushanath Babu added solemnly, "but taking one's own life should never be the answer."

***

After entering the hotel and finishing dinner, everyone quietly retreated to their rooms, weighed down by a sense of heaviness.

"I should inform Arijit now," Surya said to himself, pulling out his phone.

He called Arijit and shared the news.

"So… it's over then," Arijit responded solemnly.

"It wasn't murder. It was suicide," Surya clarified.

"Did you manage to catch those two?" Arijit asked.

"I tried everything I could, but no—I couldn't," Surya admitted.

"Keep trying. You'll get them eventually. Let's talk later," Arijit encouraged.

"Alright," Surya replied softly.

Next, he called Ujjaini to break the news.

"So, he didn't make it either…" she murmured. "He ended his own life."

"That's what happens to people who go too far down the wrong path. I'll tell you everything once I'm back in Kolkata," Surya said.

"I'll be waiting," Ujjaini replied, her voice low but steady.

***

The next morning, after breakfast, when Surya and Krishna were taking a walk outside, Shubhabrata approached them with a gentle smile and said, "Good morning."

Arpan was also by his side.

"Good morning," Surya replied.

Shubhabrata smiled faintly and said, "In the end, he chose his own path. We didn't have to do anything."

"You're right. That brings things full circle," said Surya.

"Yes, the fire that was burning inside me has finally gone out. Well then, it's time to go."

With that, the two quietly said goodbye and slowly walked away.

"Who knows where they'll go now," Krishna murmured.

"Let them go wherever their hearts lead," Surya said.

"But the ending wasn't like the Mahabharata," Krishna added, "Duryodhana was defeated by Bhima in a mace duel. But here, Bijit took his own life."

"Endings don't always follow the script," Surya said quietly. "We just have to move forward again."

***

This time, they went to Germany, and from there, they would return to Kolkata. In Germany, they visited a cuckoo clock factory nestled in the scenic Black Forest—a mountainous region steeped in charm and folklore, famously known for the inspiring fairy tales of the Brothers Grimm.

A cuckoo clock is a type of clock with a pendulum, the bell of which rings with the sound of a cuckoo. The cuckoo also comes out, flapping its wings.

"It's so beautiful. We bought one like this in Switzerland," Krishna said with admiration.

"Yes, with a cowbell attached. These clocks really seem to have a life of their own, travelling across borders," Surya added with a nostalgic smile.

But the joy of the trip slowly gave way to a heavy heart as the time came to return home. The memories were beautiful, but the sorrow of Bijit's tragic suicide hung over them like a shadow. Their return journey included a brief halt in Bahrain before finally landing in Kolkata.

"Feeling completely exhausted," Surya said as they stepped into their home. Just then, the phone rang. It was Manas da.

"Are you back?" he asked.

"Yes, we've just returned," Surya replied.

"Alright, take some rest. Arijit and I will drop by tomorrow evening," said Manas da before hanging up.

***

The old landline phone sat beside Nrisingha, its receiver worn with age. Raju, ever attentive, stayed close to care for him.

Around noon that day, the phone rang.

"Raju, see who's calling," Nrisingha said softly.

Raju picked up the receiver and said, "Hello?"

"I need to speak to Nrisingha Babu. It's important," came a voice from the other end.

"Please hold," Raju replied, and turning to Nrisingha, asked him, "Someone wants to speak with you. Should I give it to you?"

"Yes, hand it over," Nrisingha said, his hands trembling as he reached for the receiver.

"This is Shubhra—your nephew. Remember the conversation at the hospital," said Shubhabrata, his voice calm but cold.

Nrisingha said nothing.

Shubhabrata continued, "Surprised? Do you remember Arpan da? He and I took matters into our own hands. One by one, we got rid of all the sinners. First, your son-in-law, Ranajoy, then your younger son Sujit, his friend Anirban, our uncle Shamik, the wicked Animesh, and finally, it was Bijit's turn."

"What happened to Bijit?" Nrisingha asked, his voice dry and strained, "What did you do to him?"

"Worried, are you?" Shubhabrata sneered. "We didn't need to do anything. Driven by torment and guilt, he took his own life—abroad. Let this be your news for the day. You rejoiced once—now it's time to grieve. As long as you live, unrest and sorrow will be your only companions. That is your punishment."

"No, no, no," Nrisingha cried out. The receiver slipped from his hand and crashed to the floor.

***

Duryodhana, fatally wounded in battle by Bhima, had died. The news struck Dhritarashtra with unbearable sorrow—he had lost all hundred of his sons.

Sanjaya gently said, "Your Majesty, do not grieve. There is no remedy for grief—it is part of life."

But Dhritarashtra, overcome with despair, replied, "All my sons and dear friends are gone. I am blind, childless, and alone. What is left for me in this world? Why must I go on living?"

Vidura stepped forward, his voice calm and steady. "Your Majesty, rise. This is the way of the world. The dead do not return in mourning, and one cannot join them in grieving. Life must go on, even through pain."

***

"Manas da and Arijit will be here soon," said Surya.

"Everything has been arranged for them," Krishna replied. "But will you tell them everything that happened there?"

"No," Surya said calmly. "I'll tell them only what I have to say."

***

After about half an hour, the two of them arrived.

"Is everything okay?" Manas da asked.

"Absolutely fine," Surya replied.

"Now, let's get to the real point," Manas da said, lowering his voice. "Everything's just too confusing, isn't it? Surya, please explain everything."

"First, you need to read this diary," Surya said, handing it over to Manas da.

Both Manas da and Arijit began reading eagerly. As they turned the pages, the pieces began to fall into place.

"I see it now," Arijit said, glancing up. "So Dhananjaya and Vasudeva—meaning Shubhabrata and Arpan—did all this to take revenge. But where did you find this diary?"

"Someone left it outside our hotel room," Krishna answered.

Surya looked at him and added, "They wanted to expose the injustice done to them, but they didn't want to be caught. That's why they kept everything so secret."

"That makes sense," said Manas da. "But Surya, tell me—how did you get their photographs?"

Surya leaned forward. "The first thing that struck me was the weapon—bows and arrows aren't easily available. So, I began looking into places that make them. I already had photos of the arrows used. There's a shop in College Square, but they don't make this type of arrow.

"I searched in Saharanpur, Ludhiana, and several other places but found nothing. Eventually, I located the right shop in Meerut. I gathered all this information while still in Kolkata. Then I went to Meerut. When I showed the arrow photos to the shop manager, he confirmed that two Bengali men had ordered them. They even had the arrowheads specially sharpened.

"The shop had security footage, and luckily, their photos were still there. I posed as a police officer and took the images on my mobile. The names, addresses, and contact details they had provided were all fake. Then I returned to Kolkata.

"Soon after, they threatened Bijit, who fled to Hyderabad out of fear. But they managed to track him down and went after him. I saw them clearly. After landing at the airport, I returned to the hotel. Krishna, you remember that day?"

"Yes, of course. You didn't tell me where you had gone when you came back," Krishna nodded.

"I found out which hotel they were staying at. I convinced one of the staff members to secretly install a CCTV camera in their room. Through that, I tracked their movements.

"They somehow knew about Siddharth's house and guessed Bijit might go there. And they were right. I followed them there. The next day, they took Bijit's new number from Siddharth's office phone and threatened him again. It's a psychological tactic—killers often enjoy instilling fear before the act.

"Bijit panicked and fled to another location in a cab. Shubhabrata followed and scoped out the place. Then he returned to the hotel, picked up Arpan and the box containing the bow and arrows, and set off to kill him.

"That's when we intervened and brought Bijit back to Kolkata. If we hadn't, they would have killed him that very day. Even back in Kolkata, Bijit was terrified. Eventually, he decided to go to Europe, hoping the police would catch

Shubhabrata and the others by then. I had already given their photos to Arijit Babu."

"Yes," said Arijit, "and I did everything I could to catch them, but they slipped through."

"Anyway," Surya continued, "Bijit remained silent in Europe, too, possibly struggling with his own mind. Finally, unable to cope with the pressure, he took his own life. My part is done now. It's your job to catch them."

"We're working on that," said Manas Babu. "But the way you handled this entire investigation is extraordinary. You're a genius, Surya."

Surya smiled faintly. "Well, I have a proposal," he said, turning to Manas Babu.

"What kind of proposal?" Manas Babu asked.

"Let's hold a press conference and reveal everything. It'll work in your favour. No more questions, no more confusion."

"You're in charge now, Surya da," said Krishna with a grin.

"Enough of this," Surya said, chuckling. "Let's eat and drink now."

***

The next day, a press conference was held where everything was brought to light. The diary was presented, and Manas da spoke passionately about Surya's achievements, praising his courage and determination.

There was a wave of sympathy for Shubhabrata and his companion among those present.

A journalist turned to Surya and asked, "It will be better if they don't get caught. After all, they have sought justice in their own way."

Surya responded firmly, "No matter the reason, it's never right to take the law into your own hands."

***

After the press conference ended, Arijit turned to Surya and said, "No matter what you say, it seems like you actually support them morally."

Surya responded with a faint, mysterious smile.

"You're not wrong," he said. "The fact that they won public sympathy worked out brilliantly in our favour."

With the tension easing, Manas da gathered everyone and took them out to a restaurant for a celebratory treat.

***

Krishna and Surya were on their way home when Ujjaini called.

"I'll come by this afternoon," she said.

"Come on, *didi*," Krishna replied with a smile.

Ujjaini arrived later that day.

"So, the two of you just came back from Europe! Congratulations on such a huge success."

"You're a part of this success, too," Krishna said warmly.

"Oh, *baba*, that's such a sweet thing to say! Now come, I've brought chicken biryani," Ujjaini beamed.

"It's going to be delicious. And we've brought something for you too," Krishna added.

"Really?" Ujjaini asked, her eyes lighting up.

She was delighted to receive a Florentine leather bag, a Swiss watch, Swarovski crystals, and some fine Swiss chocolates. She listened with great interest as they shared stories and showed her pictures from their journey.

"I honestly hope they don't get caught," she said thoughtfully. "You know, people are aware that greed leads to trouble, yet they still give in to it and end up sinning."

"And no one escapes the consequences of their actions. Sooner or later, justice finds them," Krishna replied.

"You're right," Ujjaini nodded. "But after seeing those photos, I can't help it—I really want to visit Europe too. I feel like packing my bags right now!"

"We'll definitely go," Surya said with a grin. "But for now, let's go up to the roof and watch the sunset."

***

"The western sky is blazing with a riot of colours," Surya said mesmerised.

"Wow, that sounds like a line from a poem," Krishna said with a smile.

Just then, Kamala di arrived with a tray of ice cream.

"Chocolate ice cream!" Ujjaini exclaimed, her eyes lighting up with delight.

***

Shubhabrata and Arpan stood in an open field as heavy rain poured down around them. The downpour grew stronger with each passing moment as if the sky itself were trying to cleanse the world. It felt like all their sins and sorrows were being washed away in the rushing water. Then, after a while, the clouds slowly drifted apart, and the sun broke through, shining down with a warm, golden light.

***

"Keep this diary safe. It holds a terrible memory," Ujjaini said softly.

"Yes, you're right," Surya replied with a nod.